## "What do you want, Lucia?"

Hunter stopped a pace away to look down at her, his striking face stripped to its essential strength by the hard white light of the moon. Lucia's mouth dried; the elemental fire that burned in him banished her bleak chill in a surge of sensual heat. She felt dislocated, overwhelmed, and her emotions jerked so swiftly from one extreme to the other that she was lost.

For a moment she hesitated, torn between primitive longing and a valiant caution. Making love to Hunter would be using him....

But he wouldn't be hurt. He didn't even like her much, so it would mean nothing to him beyond easing his lust.

And oh, God, she needed warmth.

"You," she said.

*Royal Weddings*

*For richer, never poorer—*
*guaranteed scandal, passion and wealth!*

**For a Mediterranean royal family,**
**the road to the altar is paved with riches,**
**scandal and passion!**

A pregnant princess. A marriage of convenience
for a renegade prince.

Two thrilling connected stories from favorite
author Robyn Donald.

Both Princess Lucia Bagaton and Prince Guy of
Dacia are about to discover that *modern* royal
marriage isn't entirely at their command!

**This month, enjoy Princess Lucia's story.**

Look for **Prince Guy of Dacia**'s story:

*By Royal Command*
#2414

**Coming next month**
**from Harlequin Presents®!**

# Robyn Donald

## HIS PREGNANT PRINCESS

*Royal Weddings*

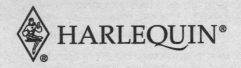

# HARLEQUIN®

TORONTO • NEW YORK • LONDON
AMSTERDAM • PARIS • SYDNEY • HAMBURG
STOCKHOLM • ATHENS • TOKYO • MILAN • MADRID
PRAGUE • WARSAW • BUDAPEST • AUCKLAND

ISBN 0-373-12408-2

HIS PREGNANT PRINCESS

First North American Publication 2004.

Copyright © 2004 by Robyn Donald.

# PROLOGUE

HUNT RADCLIFFE looked from the window of the private jet, metallic-blue eyes half-hidden by thick long lashes as he watched the desert inch past thousands of feet below. A glance at his watch confirmed that in just over an hour he'd be landing in the small Mediterranean island of Dacia.

He picked up a magazine his PA had handed over with a grin just before Hunt had boarded the plane at Capetown.

'Since when have I read society magazines?' Hunt enquired after a disbelieving glance.

The younger man's grin widened. 'I thought you might like to do some more research. It features official photographs of the Prince and Princess of Dacia at their wedding.'

Hunt already had a signed portrait of the royal couple, so he'd tossed the magazine onto an empty seat in the private jet, but now that he was almost there curiosity drove him to open it.

The formally posed shots had been taken in one of the rooms of the Dacian royal palace. Although Prince Luka and his bride, Alexa Mytton, looked cool and composed, nothing could hide the transparent happiness that radiated from them. A half-smile creased his face. No doubt, Alexa had fallen headlong in love, and it certainly looked as though the prince had met her more than halfway.

A prior engagement had kept Hunt away from the wedding, but he was now fulfilling a promise to visit his old friend and her new husband.

Hunt turned the page. His eyes met a pair of amber ones,

staring straight at the camera with the kind of haughty aloofness that set his teeth on edge.

Princess Lucia Bagaton, he read, distant cousin of the ruler of Dacia, and until his marriage his hostess.

The Ice Princess...

She was one of Alexa's bridesmaids, and by the look on that remote, beautiful face, hating every moment of it. Hunt's black brows drew together. She probably thought her precious cousin had married beneath him. God, he loathed snobbery!

With a contemptuous flick of his fingers, he tossed the magazine onto the seat beside him.

Yet a moment later he picked it up again and opened it at the same page. He'd never met Lucia Bagaton, although he'd heard enough about her from a business associate whose son had met her, fallen in love with her and eventually died because of her.

Three months previously, after the royal wedding, Hunt had kept a quiet wake with Maxime Lorraine's father as the Frenchman mourned the death of his only child. Years before, the tall New Zealander had reminded the middle-aged industrialist of himself as a young man, determined to forge a future in alien territory. Kindly Édouard Lorraine had helped Hunt negotiate the tricky protocols of European social and business arenas.

'She targeted him,' Édouard said wearily in his heavily accented English. He put his empty glass down on the side-table with a shaking hand. 'And then, when he asked her to marry him, she threw him over.'

'Snobbery?'

'Possibly. The Bagatons have a pedigree that goes back a couple of thousand years, whereas I, as you know, am a nobody. But more, I think, because of money.'

Hunt's brows shot up. 'So what was the problem?' he asked bluntly.

The older man picked up the superb cognac. 'For you too? No? I'm sure you'll grant me this indulgence for once.' He poured himself another glass, then said bleakly, 'Oh, she might have fallen in love with him, but she wanted the money more. She has none, you see. Or only a pittance.'

'I thought the Bagatons were rich,' Hunt said, frowning.

'The prince is, but her father and grandfather were charming playboys who ran through their inheritance as though they owned a goldmine. As Prince Luka's hostess she has a settled position, but when he announced his engagement to your countrywoman, Princess Lucia must have realised that her days of influence in Dacia were over. Titles, even titles as exalted as princess, are two a penny nowadays, but they do have commercial value. Looked at logically, her best bet was to find a very rich man and marry him.'

'Barter her social cachet for his money,' Hunt said with distaste.

'She has assets that push her price higher.' Édouard smiled cynically. 'That beautiful face and slim body are added value, and so is her discretion—she has figured in no scandals.'

'Have you met her?'

The older man nodded. 'Of course, as soon as Maxime told me that he had fallen in love with her I went to Dacia. She is pattern-book royalty—intelligent, exquisitely mannered, always gracious, with an endless fund of small talk.' He sipped some more of the cognac. 'I liked her very much, and it seemed to me that she liked my son, although she revealed very little of her thoughts.'

Hunt made no comment.

His host said, 'Maxime asked her to marry him the day after the Cortville deal blew up in my face. You remember it; some commentators were sure that Lorraine's would come crashing down with it.'

'I remember. They were wrong, of course.'

The older man drank half his brandy then set the glass down and finished fiercely, 'But it was touch and go for a week or so, during which the Ice Princess turned my son down. He came back shattered, and then—then he decided to join this expedition.'

Hunt frowned, but said nothing, and after a few brooding moments his host said, 'If she hadn't been so greedy, if she had waited only a few days, she could have had my son and the money, a life with as much privilege as the one she left behind. But she didn't wait and now he is dead, lost in an imbecilic attempt to discover a dinosaur in the swamps of Africa. He would never have gone if she hadn't rejected him.'

Hunt wondered. Maxime hadn't been the classic spoiled rich kid, but he'd been young enough to still feel bullet-proof. Until the break-up of his affair with the princess he'd contented himself with the usual dare-devilry, skiing the most dangerous pistes, sky-diving, racing his huge motor boat. Awash with humiliation and frustration, he'd probably jumped at the chance to go to Africa.

Now, less than an hour from meeting her, Hunt scruti-nised the lovely, aristocratic face that gazed so calmly from the magazine page. Although still intensely sorry for Édouard and angry at the waste of a young life, it was none of his business if Princess Lucia of Dacia was despicable, a woman who substituted cunning and venal self-interest for integrity.

Yet his eyes lingered on her soft red mouth, wildly pro-vocative in that aloof, controlled face.

His body stirred, hormones purring into predatory mas-culine alertness. She was truly lovely; blue highlights softened the black hair sleeked back in a regal coronet of braids, skin the softly burnished gold of a Mediterranean dawn, and eyes like a tiger's, amber with gold streaks in them...

In spite of her regal composure, Princess Lucia oozed a subtle sexuality. For years she'd been driving the gossip columnists crazy; no men in her life, no wild parties or romances, nothing but good works and self-effacement. Even her affair with Maxime hadn't reached the columns; on Dacia, her cousin had power enough to keep his family's affairs private.

He flicked over another page, and there she was again, dancing with an obviously besotted man. Beneath the photograph a cleverly worded caption wondered if this was the man in the Ice Princess's life.

Hunt said aloud, 'So she's clever, and discreet and prudent. A model princess ready to sell herself to the highest bidder.'

He had better things to do than lust over a calculating, heartless woman. Yet as he closed the magazine with a snap and tossed it onto the empty seat beside him, that exotic face, almost feline in its beauty, lingered in his mind.

It held secrets, secrets he was privy to. That gracious, seamless façade, a product of rigorous training, disguised a woman who had given herself to a man who loved her, and then cruelly spurned him.

He wondered contemptuously if she ever regretted dumping Maxime Lorraine on the strength of a rumour.

Hunt stretched his long body, a cold smile tilting the corners of his mouth. Some questions would soon be answered, because she'd be meeting him at the airport in Dacia.

# CHAPTER ONE

PRINCESS LUCIA BAGATON—known to those she loved as Cia—anchored a wisp of glossy hair behind her ears and replaced her sunglasses, her fine brows drawing together in a faint frown. Automatically her fingers went to the diamond star that rested just below the hollow of her throat. She stroked the pendant as though it was a talisman, then realised what she'd done and dropped her hand to her lap with a tightening of her lips.

Although this meeting wasn't an official occasion, she'd dressed conservatively; Hunter Radcliffe was an important figure in the business world as well as a friend of her cousin's new wife, Alexa.

In fact, Cia thought, fighting back the grey misery that had been her constant companion for months, the last person she'd met at the airport had been Alexa, now Princess Alexa of Dacia.

That meeting had changed Cia's life; this one wouldn't, but it was the last time she'd greet anyone as Luka's representative. A week from now she'd be flying away from the island, the only home she'd known since she was ten.

'We're here, your highness.' The chauffeur's voice murmured respectfully through the intercom as the limousine drew up in a private parking place out of the view of any travellers or passers-by.

'Thank you.'

Before the car stopped she'd relaxed her taut expression; the Dacians expected smiles from her. Bag clasped loosely, she waited for the elderly attendant to open the door, returned his smile and walked into the airport building.

In the private lift that led to the waiting room reserved for Dacian royal family, she asked the airport manager, 'Is Mr Radcliffe's jet on schedule?'

'It will touch down in a few minutes, your highness.'

'Good.' Another smile lilted through her words. 'Excellent, in fact. How is the new grandson?'

He looked gratified. 'A lovely little boy. And so forward! Yesterday he smiled at me—and even though my wife and daughter tell me he's far too young, it was *not* wind! I know the difference between a grimace of pain and a smile.'

Walking ahead of him out of the lift, Cia laughed. 'He must already realise that he's a lucky baby—he has a special link with his grandfather.'

She loved children. Sometimes, in the dead of another sleepless night, she mourned the children she'd never have now. Once again her hand crept to the pendant at her breast and touched the five exquisite stones that made the star. They were cold and smooth against her fingertips. Once again she dropped her hand abruptly.

The manager opened the door into the suite with a flourish. 'Well, perhaps he's a little young for that,' he conceded with a half-laugh. 'I trust everything is as you wished it, ma'am.'

Cia cast a professional glance around the room. 'It looks wonderful, as always. Thank you.'

He nodded, then looked past her out of the window. 'Ah, this must be the gentleman,' he said with satisfaction as a slender private jet touched down on the runway. 'He is a friend, I believe, of Princess Alexa's?'

'Yes. Like her, he is from New Zealand.' Her voice was very steady, as warm as she could make it—entirely normal. She'd had enough practice—Luka had been married to his lovely New Zealander for four months now. And for years before that Cia had tried to accept that he'd never see her as anything more than the much younger, very distant cousin who'd become his responsibility when she'd been orphaned.

Most people grew out of their teenage crushes, but she didn't seem to be able to chisel Luka from her heart. Loving someone for almost half of your twenty-five years was a difficult habit to break.

The sleek private jet taxied back towards the building and nestled against the end of the bridge. Firmly pinning her social secretary's smile to her mouth, Cia walked across to the gate, ready to welcome Hunter Radcliffe to Dacia.

All it needed, she thought with black humour, was for him to be in love with Alexa, and they'd have the makings of a modern novel—one of those that ended in tears and disillusion all round.

But the man she'd come to meet didn't look as though he'd ever loved anyone in his life. Watching him walk towards the gate, Cia blinked and her mouth went dry. Photographs of Hunter Radcliffe in magazines and newspapers failed to convey the formidable charisma that burned around him like an aura.

Cia swallowed. The world suddenly seemed to have become a much darker, more vital place.

Tall—taller even than Luka—with broad shoulders and lean hips and the easy, deliberate pacing of an athlete, he strode towards her like a warrior from another world. Skin burned bronze by a sun as strong as Dacia's emphasised boldly chiselled features that revealed only what their owner intended.

Neither his hard face nor narrowed eyes changed when he inspected her. Cia's stomach performed an uncomfortable manoeuvre behind her ribs.

The noisy hum of the busy airport faded. Quickly, she retrieved her slipping smile. 'Welcome to Dacia, Mr Radcliffe,' she said in English, and extended a hand. 'I'm Prince Luka's cousin—Lucia Bagaton.'

He took her hand, enveloping it in a grip judged to a nicety—firm but not crushing. The strength in his fingers and the slight calluses that indicated hard physical labour sent a swift, disturbing shiver down the length of her spine.

'How do you do, Your Highness?' He spoke in a deep, distinctive voice with a New Zealand accent, and he had definitely put capitals on the formal term of address.

Her sharp look examined a face that revealed nothing but bland politeness—if you ignored hooded, metallic-blue eyes and the twist of classically sculpted male lips.

When he continued, 'I'm pleased to be here,' she detected an edge beneath the measured courtesy of the words.

Cia had done her research; growing up motherless, like her he'd been orphaned at fourteen, spending three years in a foster home. By the time he'd reached his early twenties, Hunter Radcliffe had made a reputation on the stock market as a day trader—a route to riches that needed nerves of steel, a vast knowledge of the field, and huge amounts of luck.

Fortune duly made, he'd moved out of that incredibly risky market, expanding his interests until today he was a well-known and respected player in the world's financial scene.

Defying the unwavering impact of his gaze, she decided he was formidable enough to make a success of anything he decided to do. Sensible people probably ran for cover when his eyes, darkly blue as a dangerous midnight, probed for signs of weakness.

She couldn't—and wouldn't—run. When another ironic twist of his mouth reminded her of her manners, she held on to her steady smile. 'My cousin and Alexa send their apologies. Unfortunately they are—'

'At a special meeting of a relief organisation. I know.' He looked up as a porter wheeled his luggage through.

Not a man to waste time, she thought acidly—and with enough presence to power a large city! Why hadn't Alexa chosen to marry *him?*

Not that it would have made any difference; Cia had long been resigned to the fact that Luka would never love her the way she wanted him to.

'They'll be home by the time we get there,' she said politely, wondering if Hunter Radcliffe normally greeted strangers with barely restrained aggression.

Possibly; you didn't rise from his background to become a tycoon unless you were tough and forceful and ruthless, and of course, once you reached his heights you could be as rude as you liked to almost anyone without worrying about the consequences.

As if she cared! In her most courteous voice she said, 'Ah, here are your bags. I'm afraid you'll have to go through Customs and Immigration before we can leave.'

Five minutes later, his passport stamped and his luggage whisked off to the waiting limousine, she indicated the door. 'This way.'

He stood back to let her go out first. 'After you, Your Highness.' A faint, infuriating note of mockery coloured the words.

Straight-backed, Cia preceded him into the corridor. Either he'd taken an instant dislike to her, or he disapproved of the monarchy. It was a method of governance many believed to be on its way out, but try and convince the Dacians of that! After long, terrifying years protected from the territorial ambitions of a neighbouring dictator solely by their prince's marriage to the tyrant's only child, they weren't planning to give up their loyalty to the Bagaton family in the near future.

And she didn't care what this man thought of her. It was surprising, though, that Alexa, who was a darling, should have such a coolly arrogant friend.

At the lift, Cia reached for the button, startled when a lean, tanned hand forestalled her automatic summons. She looked up, and met eyes so piercing she had to stop herself from taking a betraying step backwards. A pulse jumped in her throat and swift, unexpected heat licked the width of her cheekbones as her hand dropped.

The lift doors opened in sighing welcome. Gratefully she stiffened her shoulders and walked in.

Glancing at the control panel, Hunter Radcliffe observed, 'I assume we're heading for the ground floor.' Then added, 'Your Highness,' again edging each word with that flick of sarcasm.

'Yes,' she said shortly.

He pressed the button and the lift began its descent. It was idiotic to let herself be so affected by him.

It was the colour of his eyes, she decided. In Dacia liquid darkness reined supreme, and she was accustomed to the signature tawny-gold of the Bagaton family. Alexa had crystalline grey eyes, and although Cia's English relatives came equipped in various shades of blue, none drilled through her defences like lasers.

Did Hunter Radcliffe's ever warm up? Making love, perhaps...

A suspect surge of adrenalin sharpened her senses. She stared stonily ahead, uncomfortably aware of the faint, vital scent of the man beside her.

Who moved slightly, and smiled down at her. It was a killer smile—sexy, disturbing and mercifully brief. Her stomach lurched again, then contracted into a tight knot.

Fuming and oddly disoriented, Cia clung to her dignity as her composure began to splinter.

'I don't think I've ever been in a lift reserved for royalty until now,' he observed.

Cia forced a tight smile. 'It's actually for private visitors,' she corrected.

He seemed to fill the lift, dominating it as he'd dominated the waiting room, without effort.

It's called presence, she told herself crossly. He had it in spades.

Clad casually in cotton trousers and a shirt that revealed broad shoulders and a splendid chest, the man made her feel ineffectual and ridiculously formal. No silk dress—not even a bronze one that made her skin and eyes glow—could compete with his impact.

It will be interesting, Cia thought loyally, to see him with Luka. Two uncompromising men, both accustomed to power…

As the lift gained momentum she summoned a smile and said lightly, 'It isn't necessary to call me Your Highness. Even in formal situations it's only used once, and after that a simple ma'am will do. Informally, most people just call me Lucia.'

'Thank you for telling me that,' he said gravely.

Cia looked up sharply. When his lips curved into a smile that combined speculation with a taunt, she realised that she hadn't told him anything he didn't know. Hunter Radcliffe rubbed shoulders with the world's power élite, so he'd have learned the intricacies of formal address.

Chagrin chipped away at her crumbling self-possession. She should have realised—she *would* have realised if she hadn't been thrown off balance by his attitude!

Pinning a professional smile in place, she straightened the

diamond star on its chain and dropped it inside the neck of her dress. It looked like being a long week.

Surely the lift was much slower than usual? She seemed to have been shut in it with this overbearing, sarcastic man for hours.

In that distinctive voice, he drawled, 'You'll have to forgive me for any mistakes I might make. In New Zealand we don't often meet royalty.'

Well, two could play at that game. Anticipation simmering through her veins, she countered sweetly, 'Oh, don't worry about it—Kiwis are clearly very adaptable people. Alexa has managed superbly. And I'm sure she told me you had some order or another—I'm sorry, I can't remember which—bestowed on you by your Queen? Perhaps she was wrong?'

His brows drew together in a swift, formidable frown. 'Alexa must keep up with the newspapers from home.'

The lift drew to a stop on the ground floor with Cia savouring a moment's wicked satisfaction. Her delicate insinuation that he'd been bragging to Alexa had grazed his formidable self-possession. Still, she wasn't going to let him off the hook so swiftly, and if the wind-chill factor fell any lower, she'd just wear winter clothes.

'And I'm sure I've seen photographs of you escorting— oh, a princess from another European royal house,' she murmured discreetly, donning her sunglasses like a shield before they emerged into the blinding Dacian sunlight. The doors opened in front of them.

'I didn't expect you to be an eager follower of the gossip columns,' Hunter parried, his voice smooth as silk.

She bestowed a pleasant smile on him. 'I'm related to almost every royal family in Europe, and, as in all families, news travels fast,' she said easily. The princess—her cousin—had confided that he was a magnificent lover.

Even without inside information, Cia would have guessed. His potent male magnetism proclaimed his sexual expertise. But she'd been surprised—and a little sceptical—when the cousin had gone on to say that he'd been faithful while they'd been together.

'This way,' Cia said, automatically indicating the waiting limousine.

Once the limousine doors were closed, the man sitting beside her settled his broad shoulders back into the seat and surveyed her with his particular brand of challenging speculation. 'What exactly do you do here, ma'am? Good works?'

'My name is Lucia,' she said, hiding the sudden heat in her blood with another expertly controlled smile. 'As for what I do—nothing.' And waited for the familiar pain.

It didn't arrive; instead she was zinging with irritation and a kind of reluctant, abrasive awareness.

His sardonic glance cut through her composure. Bewildered by the strength of her anger—with him and with herself for reacting to his unspoken contempt—she added, 'I used to be the palace social secretary.'

Handsome didn't apply to Hunter Radcliffe; the word was too wishy-washy to describe the strong, thrusting bone structure that gave his face such authority. And he didn't possess Luka's spectacular male beauty.

But his was not a face she'd ever forget. Arrogantly compelling, his features gave him a kind of ruthless, patient concentration that made the name Hunter fit him exactly. Although his self-control blazed like a cold beacon, she sensed he'd make a bad enemy.

He turned a simple response like the raising of his black brows into a subtle insult. 'Social secretary? It sounds a riveting career.'

Resolutely Cia kept her face set in an expression of calm

detachment. Not only had he decided he didn't like her, he was making sure she knew it. 'Somebody has to do it, and it was one way I could help Luka.'

'Why did he need help?'

She said briskly, 'He didn't need help—he needed an efficient, reliable organiser.'

'And his need was a good enough reason for you to dedicate your life to smoothing his social path?'

Cia shrugged. 'My mother died when I was ten, and my father wasn't very interested in me, so Luka made sure I spent every school holiday here, and when I left school I came to live here.'

He nodded. 'I thought you had English relatives.'

'They weren't very interested either,' she said evenly. 'Luka and Guy, another Bagaton cousin, made me feel I had a family, but I knew Luka best.'

His acceptance and affection had been a novelty for a girl who'd been the third wheel in a spectacularly unsuccessful marriage. She added lamely, 'I was glad to repay him in whatever way I could.'

Although Hunter was glancing at the passing scenery, she had an impression of a cold, clever mind sifting and sorting facts. Let him think what he wants, she thought scornfully; she didn't care a fig for his opinion.

'I gather the boarding-school was in England,' he startled her by observing. When Cia's brows lifted he went on, 'That would explain your faultless accent.'

Not without satisfaction she replied, 'That, and the fact that my mother was English.'

'So your colouring came from your father.'

The invisible hairs on the nape of her neck lifted in instinctive warning. 'Not entirely,' she said with remote courtesy. 'My mother was part-French and I look like her, but of course black hair and brown eyes are standard in the Mediterranean.'

'Possibly, but skin the colour and texture of pale gold satin, and eyes like hot amber are not.' The words emerged in an abrasive male purr, sensuous yet controlled.

Although the air-conditioning was on, the inside of the car suddenly seemed oppressively humid. Sweat sprang out across her temples; without thinking, Cia touched the chain around her neck, her fingers sliding down to clasp the diamond star.

She flushed when Hunter's blue gaze followed the betraying little movement, and released the pendant, folding her hand firmly in her lap. This man, she thought disjointedly, is dangerous.

It took every ounce of self-possession to say, 'You have an interesting line in compliments. Hot amber—I must remember that. I don't think the Bagaton eyes have ever been described like that before. And I like the idea of skin like golden satin too.' She managed a smile, coolly distant. 'It might make the constant application of sunscreen less irritating. It's the predominant scent of the Mediterranean in summer—sunscreen.'

She surprised a cynical laugh out of him. 'Not yours. When you walk there's a faint drift of very exclusive perfume and a soft whisper of silk. As for your skin—you must know that every man who sees it wonders how it would look against his.'

Awareness, sharp and reckless, clamoured through her body in sensations so powerfully narcotic that she had to stop herself from squirming on the seat. She should give him a disdainful glance and turn the conversation, but she didn't trust her voice.

Silence drummed between them. In the end she managed

a smile that was, she hoped, both amused and repressive, and said, 'I'm afraid I didn't know that until you told me.'

Until the moment she'd seen Hunter Radcliffe walk into the airport she'd had no idea that she could feel a lethal, violent attraction for a man she didn't know and was rapidly learning to dislike. As its dark intensity shafted through her, she realised she had no way of dealing with him. Armoured against all other men by her love for Luka, at twenty-five she was still a virgin.

A virgin turned on by this man! *Live Dangerously* had been the motto of one of her ancestors—it certainly wasn't hers.

Either he was as big a womaniser as the gossip columnists hinted, or he felt that same driving lure. His blue eyes had heated to glinting jewels in his tanned face, and the smile sculpting his wide, sensual mouth was definitely, if reluctantly, appreciative.

Savage, undiluted excitement sizzled through her body. Trying to douse it with common sense, Cia commanded herself trenchantly to grow up. With that indefinable air of sexual charisma, and his power and the money that went with it, he'd had women falling at his feet ever since he'd made the world stage. Probably before; he didn't need money or position to attract attention.

She jutted her chin, frowning when she saw a child trudging along the road ahead. Through the intercom she said, 'Julio, stop, please.'

'Your highness?'

'We'll give her a lift,' she said briskly, ignoring Hunter Radcliffe's quizzical expression.

As soon as the car stopped she got out. 'Well, little one,' she said in Dacian, 'what are you doing away from school?'

The child—no more than six or seven—shrank back until she recognised who had stopped her. Knuckling her eyes, she flung herself into Cia's arms and burst into tears. Cia fished out a handkerchief and set to the business of comforting.

When the swift storm had passed, she coaxed the child into the car and soon extracted the story from her.

It was long and involved, and there were more sobs before it was told, but Cia finally removed her arm from around the thin shoulders and said, 'There, that's enough now, Gracia. Blow your nose again, and wipe your eyes. I think I should take you home and perhaps chat to your mother.'

With a worshipful smile Gracia obeyed, but before the car had gone far she turned to stare up at Hunter. To Cia's surprise he grinned at the child, a humorous flash of white teeth that summoned a shy smile in answer.

'Good morning, miss,' he said in very passable Dacian.

The child giggled and Hunter winked at her, then looked across the small black head to meet Cia's startled eyes. His smile faded as their gazes collided.

Cia's heart jumped in her chest and that suspicious tide of sensation began another rampage. Humiliated by her lack of control, she released herself from the steel-blue trap and gazed stubbornly ahead.

At least he wasn't going to be here long. This time next week he'd have left Dacia.

And so will you, taking off to London to wallow in self-pity and mourn a love you never had, she thought in astringent self-contempt, and began to talk to their small passenger, who reached up and touched the pendant at her breast with a grubby, wondering finger.

'It's so pretty,' the child whispered. 'My mummy has a cross, but it doesn't shine like this.'

'It was a birthday present from the prince,' Cia told her. She glanced up and found Hunt examining the star with hard interest. In English she said, 'How much Dacian do you speak?'

'I can greet and farewell,' he told her, 'with a few other phrases.'

'I see. I told her that my cousin gave it to me for my eighteenth birthday.'

'A very suitable gift,' Hunter Radcliffe said, not looking at it. 'Excellent stones.'

The car drew up outside a small, stone house and Cia said evenly, 'I'll go in with her and tell her mother what's happened.'

Hunt nodded and said to the child, 'God go with you.'

The little girl giggled again at the formal farewell, but said in a low voice, 'And you, sir.'

Hunt watched them disappear into the house, the child skipping along with her hand in Cia's, the princess very much in charge.

Security on Dacia obviously wasn't much of an issue; although the driver got out and gazed around, he wasn't on full alert.

Hunt opened the door and stepped onto the road, drawing in a deep breath of sweet, scented air. He shouldn't be surprised that Princess Lucia was so good with children. That was what female royalty did; smiled a lot, accepted bouquets of flowers from kids, and learned how to make small talk in their cradle.

He hoped Alexa enjoyed it. He also hoped that her husband realised he'd married a real artist with a camera, not just another amateur.

And he hoped to hell he didn't see much of Princess Lucia during the next week. Normally well disciplined, his hormones had rioted into uncomfortable life the moment he'd laid eyes on her, so cool and composed, every hair ruthlessly organised into that sleek bun at the back of her head, her golden gaze remote and assured.

He set his analytical mind to working out just what about her had tugged at the leash on his self-control. Beauty, of course, but he'd seen enough beautiful women to be able to appreciate them without wanting to get them into bed.

And yeah, there was something sleekly tactile about that golden skin, and that trick of lowering her long lashes and then looking up through them sang straight through his defences. Couple that with a soft mouth that suggested a secret voluptuousness wildly at odds with her restrained exterior, and the predator inside him stretched its claws and sniffed the air.

Add a slender body in the right proportions and a smooth voice that went from cool English to warm, soft Dacian, and you had feminine dynamite.

His eyes narrowed. No wonder Maxime had fallen for her.

He watched as she emerged from the house, the child's hand still in hers, the white-aproned mother, with another child in her arms and one at her feet, beaming effusively.

Hunt's body sprang into red alert. Hot Dacian sunlight glowed lovingly across the princess's patrician face, hinted at the soft curves of breasts and narrow waist, the rhythmic movement of her hips as they came up to the car.

His hand clenched on the door as he opened it and got in.

The driver opened the door for her and listened with an expressionless face while she gave him some directions.

As the engine started, Cia gave a cool smile to the man sitting beside the little girl. 'We're taking Gracia back to school.'

The child twinkled up at him, and got that shockingly disarming grin once more.

Hunter said, 'She ran away?'

'She'd rather be at home with her mother and the two little ones.'

'But a royal decree did the trick,' he said softly.

'I promised that if she goes to school every day she isn't ill, Alexa would visit her school at the end of the year and present the attendance certificates.'

Recognising the name of her princess, Gracia turned to Hunter and burst out, 'She is like a fairy princess! I saw her ride in a carriage in her white wedding dress with the prince—she is so beautiful.'

Despising herself for a faint, sour twist of jealousy, Cia translated, before adding in Dacian, 'She won't come to the school in her wedding clothes, but she will wear a pretty dress.'

Hunter said, 'Would you mind telling Gracia that if she stays at school every day, I'll send her a book about New Zealand?'

Gracia beamed and wanted to know where this strange country was, so the rest of the trip was taken up with a three-way conversation in two languages.

When Cia was back in the car, being waved off by the entire class, Hunter Radcliffe said admiringly, 'That was a clever bit of PR. I hope Alexa doesn't mind you making appointments for her.'

Biting back her outrage, Cia gave a last wave to the excited children. 'I'm sure she won't—she knows how important education is for every child.' She changed the subject with considerably less than her usual finesse. 'Luka tells me that you have an interest in forest rehabilitation, Mr Radcliffe.'

'My name is Hunter.'

She paused, then repeated in a colourless voice, 'Hunter.'

'But most people call me Hunt.'

When she remained stubbornly silent he observed, 'As I'm sure you've found out from Alexa, New Zealanders are informal. But determined.'

'Hunt,' she said between her teeth. And suspected that her *hot amber* gaze told him how very appropriate she considered both his full name and the shortened version to be.

## CHAPTER TWO

EYES burnished blue as starfire beneath outrageously long lashes, Hunt gave her a smile that skimmed the borders of mockery. 'And yes, I am very interested in forest rehabilitation.'

Cia said doggedly, 'Was there any particular incident that started you off in this field?'

The man beside her fixed his gaze on the hills of Dacia, dark with the trees planted by Luka's father. 'I bought a station in—'

'Station?' She looked enquiringly at him.

'A cattle station,' he enlarged.

'What is the difference between a farm and a station?'

'A station is bigger—often much bigger—than a farm. It's usually on poorer, steeper country, further from civilisation, and whereas farms can produce a variety of produce, stations are usually pastoral—that is, their business is producing food from animals. More than you wanted to know?'

He was giving her a chance to repay his rudeness. Armoured by propriety, Cia managed to resist temptation, but it was a close-run thing. She'd met a range of people in her life, some difficult, some rude, some snobbish; none of them had managed to make her bristle as much as this man. 'Local idioms are very interesting. Is this station your home? Alexa said you live in Northland.'

'I do. The place I'm referring to is several hundred miles further south—steep country stripped of its original cover of bush and rapidly eroding into the sea.'

Cia nodded. 'So naturally you planted it with trees. Did

27

you choose ones native to that area, or exotic species?' Rather pleased at her smooth, interested tone, she risked an upward glance.

Only to find him surveying her with sardonic understanding; he knew exactly what she was doing. Her heart lurched and missed a beat, but she forced herself to meet those far too perceptive eyes with limpid innocence.

'I chose exotic trees in the most eroded spots because they grow faster, but all the gullies were fenced and replanted with native trees,' he informed her.

Cia gazed blindly out of the window, trying to ignore the deep, potent voice and concentrate on what he was saying. She'd trained herself to concentrate on people who spoke to her, but this man managed to scramble the circuits in her brain so that all she was aware of was his voice, cool and steady with an intriguingly abrasive thread running beneath it.

Startled when he stopped, she flung more words into the small silence. 'Luka's father planted trees here when he realised the soil on the hills was washing down to the sea. It's worked well.'

'He was ahead of his time,' Hunt observed laconically. 'I'm sure I'm boring you—you don't have to make small talk.'

Infuriating though he was, for the first time in months—since she'd realised that Luka loved Alexa—energy rushed through her in an exhilarating surge. And despising herself didn't curb her response; it had nothing to do with her mind or her emotions.

Hunter—*Hunt*—Radcliffe had a powerfully physical effect on her.

Instead of the platitude she'd normally have produced, she murmured, 'Oh, don't worry—small talk is a vital part of my job.'

He showed his teeth—very white, she noticed—in a grin that warned her she was out of her depth. 'Does that mean being bored—or boring people are part of your job?'

'Both,' she said lightly.

That ironic smile narrowed. 'It sounds like hell—coping with boredom, or with people who bore you, while hoping you're not boring them. Why don't you get yourself a proper job?'

'But I meet such fascinating people in this one,' she purred, tawny eyes gleaming.

He flung back his head and laughed with open enjoyment. That suspicious energy surged up another gear, tightening into an acute tension. Cia could have closed her eyes and drawn from memory everything about him—the arrogant jut of his hawkish features, the blade of a nose, the high, savage cheekbones and the ruthless line of his jaw.

As for the disturbing combination of raw strength, discipline and male promise that was his mouth, she suspected it would haunt her for a long time.

'You weren't boring me,' he said lazily. 'I like the way your mouth moves when you talk and the way you use your lashes—are tricks like that all part of the job too?'

No doubt about it, he's a brilliant lover, she thought dazedly.

She endured his piercing gaze for as long as she could, aware with some primal instinct that this was a surrender of sorts. When his eyes narrowed further she realised she was touching Luka's pendant, her fingertips caressing the five superb diamonds that made up the star.

Heat prickled through her, but she lowered her hand in a casual movement and said collectedly, 'The main part of my job is to be inconspicuous.'

'Inconspicuous?' He lifted his brows and surveyed her face with such lazy thoroughness that her hands itched to slap him even while that forbidden sizzle burned through her nerves.

'With that face you'd be conspicuous in a harem,' he drawled.

Disgusted with herself for reacting like a hot-blooded adolescent, she said colourlessly, 'You're too kind,' and grabbed the conversation by the scruff of its neck, firmly re-routing it in a safer direction by pointing out items of interest.

He must have decided that goading her was no longer amusing, because he leaned back with a satirical half-smile, as they passed stone-walled olive orchards. Spring had dusted the grass beneath the branches with a riotous crop of golden crocuses and cobalt grape hyacinths that blended into clouds of irises and brilliant marigolds.

In spite of her taut awareness, Cia discovered that she was enjoying the drive. He had a formidable mind. But then, he was a formidable man—compelling, forceful and too sure of himself.

Remembering Alexa's interest in antiquities, she indicated a church built over the ruins of a Roman temple. 'This is the old road from the port to a Roman emperor's villa in the hills. We're not going to the Old Palace in the city; it's mostly used for ceremonial purposes. Luka and Alexa actually live in the Little Palace, a much more intimate house a few kilometres in the hills. It's cooler there, with lovely gardens.'

Hunt listened to her soft, low voice, his unruly senses stirring at the subtle cadences and the silken, sensuous undernote through each word. Usually his cold, analytical brain could override the urging of his hormones, but this woman's potent allure had pressed every button.

Now he understood why Maxime Lorraine had fled civilisation when she'd turned him down. It was probably the first time the handsome heir to the Lorraine fortune had ever met rejection, and the shock and humiliation would have been impossible for him to bear. Hunt's lip curled. According to the letter Maxime had left before taking off for the Congo, she'd led him on, convincing him that she reciprocated his feelings.

The princess's voice broke into Hunt's thoughts. 'I believe you're an old friend of Alexa's?'

'I've known her since she was a skinny sixteen-year-old in love with a camera.'

No emotion registered in her sultry eyes, set like tawny jewels between thick black lashes. 'She's still in love with it—she has donated some magnificent photographs to an international exhibition that's raising funds for charity.'

When they left the main road and began to wind upwards, Hunt looked out of the window without seeing anything of the passing landscape.

He'd met hundreds of beautiful women in his life. Some—a rare few—had possessed characters that matched their faces. He suspected that Édouard had been correct; this one had had the heart of a siren, cold and scheming and avaricious.

'Exactly how closely related to the prince are you?' he asked lazily.

'Very distantly,' she said on a flat note that warned him she resented the question.

Tough. 'But you're close enough to be a princess?'

'Continental usage differs from English. My great-grandfather was the second son of the then ruler of Dacia. All of his descendants can claim the title.'

'How many other princesses and princes of Dacia are running around the world's fleshpots?'

She sent a shaft of golden fire in his direction. 'My cousin Guy is the only other one, and although he probably knows a fleshpot when he sees one, he spends most of his time looking after his business affairs,' she told him, her polite tone barely hiding her annoyance.

'Are only three of you left?'

Sunlight gleamed on her hair as she nodded. 'Quite a few of them died in various wars, but my forebears weren't prolific.'

'You said you're related to every royal family in Europe.'

Her luscious mouth curved in a humourless pretence at a smile. 'Very distantly,' she told him. 'Ah, here we are.'

Hunt leaned back while the sentries checked them through the gates. He approved the discreet surveillance as they drove through a park towards the Little Palace.

Italian in conception, the Little Palace was a large, glorious confection in stone the colour of good champagne. When the car stopped at the bottom of a magnificent flight of steps an attendant hurried to open the door and two people walked between the columns and came down towards them.

As always when she saw her cousin, Cia's heart contracted, but now she felt awkward and constrained by the presence of the man next to her. For some reason she'd be utterly humiliated if Hunter—Hunt—Radcliffe found out that she was hopelessly in love with Luka.

Alexa was looking a little tired, but she greeted them with her bright, warm smile, reaching up to kiss Hunt's cheek before introducing him to her husband. Both big men, both with indefinable charisma and authority in their different ways, they shook hands. One glance was enough to tell Cia that they liked each other.

A wave of loneliness took her by surprise, and she thought suddenly, I'll be glad to leave Dacia.

As soon as she'd realised that Luka loved Alexa she'd wanted to run as far and as fast as she could, but loyalty—

and protocol—had forced her to stay. He'd asked her to help his new wife find her way around the business of being a princess and she couldn't let Luka down—or the woman he loved.

It had been slow torture grinding away her soul, but even now, although everything was arranged and she was determined to go, the thought of only ever coming back as a guest clawed at her heart.

But Alexa had settled into island life with disarming ease and an innate dignity and discretion that would stand her in good stead. Quick-witted and sunny, she'd already captured the islanders' hearts, and court officials automatically went to their new princess.

Alexa turned to her. 'Thank you so much for collecting Hunt.'

'It was nothing,' Cia said promptly, keeping any hint of malice from her voice.

She looked up and saw Hunt watching her, his cold eyes narrowed and intent. An odd sensation in the pit of her stomach coalesced into a feverish, unknown excitement. Bestowing him a prim, cool smile, she went with them out of the sun into the elegance of the Little Palace.

Lunch was a cheerful, informal occasion. Luka had to leave early to attend another meeting, and shortly afterwards Cia excused herself on the pretext of doing some work. As she left the comfortable sitting room in the private apartments, she heard Alexa say something, followed by Hunt's deep, sexy laugh.

A familiar chill of alienation brushed Cia's spine as she walked up the stairs. Shivering, she shut the office door behind her and sat down at the desk to turn on her computer.

Some hours later she closed down the computer and got up to walk across to the window, staring down at the harmonious glory of the gardens, their classical proportions brightened by a riot of flowers from lilies to bougainvillea, glowing like stained glass amongst the soothing greenery.

Surely she'd get over this embarrassing, tormenting anguish of love? Like most women, she wanted a happy marriage, and she loved children.

Unfortunately she wanted them to be Luka's.

The sound of the door opening swivelled her around. Her heart jumped when she saw the long, lean form of her cousin.

'Hello,' she said cheerfully. 'Finished your meeting?'

'Yes.' Unsmiling, he came across the room, stopping so that he could examine her face. 'You look sad,' he said quietly. 'You looked sad before, too. What is it, Cia?'

Her mind raced, but she couldn't answer. He waited until the silence stretched too far, then said, 'You can tell me, Cia. You know that I love you, and no matter what has happened, I will support you. Is it a man?'

Oh, Luka! Emotions ran raw and angry through her. Desperately, she said, 'No, of course it's not a man. I'm feeling a bit sentimental. I've just finished the last bit of official work I had to do, and it's hitting home that in a week's time I'll have left Dacia.'

Luka was watching her closely, but at her words he relaxed and held out his hand. 'I know how to deal with that. Alexa gets homesick still.'

If she accepted the comfort he was offering she'd fling herself into his arms and bawl her eyes out. She'd kept her secret for years; she wasn't going to reveal it at the last moment.

She said, 'Once I'm away I'll enjoy myself, but at the moment I'm remembering all the things I love about Dacia and I'm in a very delicate state! I warn you, touch me, and I'll burst into tears.' Sheer inspiration produced her next words. 'And I refuse to turn up at dinner with red eyes and a red tip to my nose. Hunter Radcliffe already thinks I'm an inbred parasite with a brain the strength of soufflé and a love of the easy life. I refuse to let him think I cry.'

That convinced Luka. Laughing, he let his hand fall. 'So you like him?'

'I think he's an autocratic pig,' she returned, adding with a wicked smile, 'However, he's a very attractive, autocratic pig. Although pig is probably the wrong word too—he reminds me of something very feline, very powerful and untamed. I owe it to all princesses to keep my end up.'

Luka's brows drew together. 'I'm not sure that he's a good man to challenge.'

'Perish the thought!' She produced a wide smile. 'Pride demands that I don't let him get away with being so judgemental.' And when he continued to frown she went on, 'Luka, I'm not planning to run away with him! He has to be a reasonably decent sort or he wouldn't be a friend of Alexa's, but I don't think I like him. Of course, that might be because for some reason he thinks I'm a prissy parasite.'

'I doubt that very much,' Luka said drily, and glanced at his watch. 'I'll see you at dinner.'

When she was alone again she sagged, and her fingers came up to clutch the star on its gold chain. With a twisted grimace she let it drop.

Perhaps, to make sure neither Luka nor Alexa realised how much she was dreading her departure, she would flirt a little with Hunt Radcliffe tonight.

It would be exhilarating crossing swords with him, and not at all dangerous, because he was tough enough not to take a woman's advances seriously.

Not, she thought sadly, like poor Maxime, who had fallen headlong into love with her and when she'd tactfully turned his proposal down, had been outraged, forcing her to endure a wretched scene when he'd pleaded, then got angry and ended up calling her ugly names before storming out.

She swallowed. That final scene had been utterly distasteful, but she'd been appalled a few weeks later to read of his death. Such a waste.

Later, when the warm, lazy afternoon was on the cusp of evening, she changed into a sleek dress the colour of dark chocolate, and reapplied her make-up, sweeping her hair back from her face. Frowning, she hesitated over the star, but wore it because, she told herself, it matched the diamond stud earrings that had been an inheritance from her mother.

Normally she'd have worn plain shoes; tonight an unusual whim persuaded her to slip on a pair of high-heeled sandals.

'Well, all right, so the wretched man looms over you,' she muttered at her reflection in the long mirror. 'An extra couple of inches isn't going to make much difference.'

But she regretted that spurt of defiance when she walked out from the palace and through the parterre with its low clipped hedges. The path was level and well-rolled, but not suitable for fashionable sandals.

Halfway down the axis of the garden she looked up and saw a tall figure emerge from a walk shaded by dark, clipped conifers. Her pulse rate picked up speed when she recognised the loose, graceful stride. Austere in black and white evening clothes, Hunt overwhelmed her.

Rallying, she thought indignantly that most men his size could only aim to be rangy. However well-tailored their suits, men as tall and broad as Hunt looked either blocky and solid like bodyguards, or clumsy. Instead, he was breathtaking, the cool elegance of his clothes reinforced and strengthened by uncompromising power, both physical and mental.

Her mouth dried and she had to swallow so she'd be able to say something when she reached him.

He stopped and waited for her to come up, his lean, striking face angular in the soft dusk, unnerving her with his stillness.

The hairs on Cia's skin lifted uncomfortably. Jumpy as a cat caught in a thunderstorm, she managed, 'Good evening,' in a light, pleasant tone as she reached him.

'Good evening.' His words were abrupt and unaccompanied by anything like a smile.

Stung, she said crisply, 'Someone should have shown you where to—'

'Someone tried, but I didn't need them.' He turned to go with her down a broad flight of stairs into a lower garden. 'Am I late?'

'No, I'm early. We're dining at the summer house, so I'm just going to make sure everything's all right.'

'Summer house? That's a very English term.'

Responding to the thread of amusement in his deep voice, Cia confided in her best social tone, 'Wait until you see it! In the late nineteenth century one of the ancestors decided he wanted a summer house after a visit to England. So he built one.'

Everything about this woman set his teeth on edge; Hunt felt a slow simmer of anger at his blatant response to her. Each time he saw her—or thought of her—his testosterone levels soared off the monitor, forcing him to fight a hunger that came from a much more primal level than insipid attraction.

He wanted her, and he wanted her now, and he wanted her in all the ways a man could want a woman, including some that hadn't been invented yet. Even thinking about her stressed his self-control severely; walking beside her in the soft warmth of a Mediterranean dusk with the lazy, erotic scent of flowers floating on the air just about shattered it.

What thoughts hid behind that lovely, controlled face? That his blood was unsuitably red, not royally blue?

He hadn't got where he was by giving in to his baser desires; his hunger for Princess Lucia was purely physical, the instinctive reflex of a male animal when it encountered a receptive female ready for mating.

And as he was not an animal, he was damned well going to control it—even though he knew she was acutely aware of him. As a valet had unpacked his clothes he'd toyed with the idea of making her suffer a little for her cruel rejection of Maxime, only to dismiss it. He had no right to revenge. Besides, she was merely playing the marriage game according to the rules of her class.

Which sounded, he thought now, suspiciously as though he was making excuses for her behaviour.

One of her ridiculously high heels slid off a pebble and she faltered; his hand shot out to grasp her by the elbow. She teetered on the edge of balance and he pulled her upright, supporting her warm, curved form against his.

She froze. He looked down at her startled face, forcing himself to ignore the sudden clamour in his body. Which way would she go? If he bent his head and made himself master of that lush, sensuous mouth she'd respond—but would it be with a smile or a slap? Or both?

'Thank you—I'm fine,' she said breathlessly, stepping away and marching off down the garden without a backwards glance.

But not before Hunt had noted a blaze of colour along her cheekbones. He caught her up in a couple of strides, and fought back the uncivilised instinct to snatch her up, drag her into the shadow of the huge conifers on either side of the path, and kiss her senseless.

In a sardonic voice he observed, 'If you must wear entirely unsuitable shoes—however much they show off your magnificent legs and pretty ankles—arm yourself with a footman. Or a walking stick.'

She sent him an acid glance but didn't reply, and they walked the rest of the way in a silence thick with tension. From the corner of his eye Hunt noticed her spine, straight and true as a rod of steel, but she kept her lovely face under strict discipline.

Outside a marble fantasy that bore a strong resemblance to a Roman forum, Hunt stopped and surveyed it with slowly rising brows. 'You call this a summer house? It doesn't look like any summer house I've ever seen,' he observed drily.

Her gurgle of laughter sounded genuinely amused—and infuriatingly erotic. 'He also built a replica of a Greek temple on one of the beaches. Luka says he was obsessed by delusions of grandeur, but I think he was a raging romantic.'

'Does it run in the family?'

She walked up the marble steps and through large wooden doors studded with bosses of dark bronze. The room inside held a long table, exquisitely set with candles and flowers. Hunt, who had attended his share of banquets, deduced from the colourful china and linen that this dinner was to be informal.

'Oh, we're all very practical now,' she said flatly, casting an expert eye over the table. 'That's the thing about monarchies—the ones that don't learn to adapt lose their jobs.'

'Your family has adapted well,' he commented. 'The prince has made his mark in the cut-throat world of international banking and your cousin Guy heads one of the most innovative software firms in the world.'

'Yes,' Lucia said colourlessly. Apparently satisfied with the state of the table, she indicated the colonnade that marked the other side of the summer house. 'If you want to see why my several times great-grandfather built here, come outside.'

The columns led onto more steps, shallow and semicircular and thence to a wide, stone-flagged area where chairs and loungers had been placed to take advantage of the view. A fountain shimmered in one corner, softly caressing the air with its music.

Hunt considered himself completely blasé about the pretty things the very rich surrounded themselves with; he'd spent time in many of the world's beauty spots and lived in one of the most beautiful of all, yet something about this place stopped him in his tracks.

White-flowered vines draped the stone balustrade that seemed to project out into soft blue-hazed emptiness. When he walked beside Lucia across the terrace, a heady, far from subtle perfume surrounded them. His gaze traversed a huge lounger, plenty big enough for two.

That Victorian ancestor might have had delusions of grandeur, he thought ironically, but he'd designed this place as a seduction pad. And he'd bet his last dollar that even nowadays servants and gardeners were actively discouraged from coming here.

Lucia stopped, resting her elegant hands on the balustrade, and looked out across a great scoop of countryside, dim in the falling dusk. On the horizon the lights of Dacia's main city looped like a necklace around the harbour.

'That's the port,' she said, her voice cool and remote. 'In the daytime you can see out over farms and trees and orchards—it looks like something from a mediaeval painting.'

'My house looks out over a view like this,' Hunt told her. 'Only there's no port, no villages, no lights. And once you reach the sea, it's empty all the way to Chile apart from a few interruptions like Tahiti and Easter Island. It doesn't look at all like a mediaeval painting.'

'It sounds wonderful,' she said pleasantly. 'Like the last frontier.'

The balustrade was warm from the sun, but the heat smouldering through her was caused solely by Hunt Radcliffe. The view shimmered into a haze; she couldn't concentrate on anything but him. From the corner of her eye she saw him grip the stone edge a few inches away from her. Her heart started that crazy thudding she'd felt when he'd held her against him for those shocking, unpredictable moments.

Long-fingered, strong, his hands were those of a man who worked hard for a living. They had supported her with a confident ease that melted her bones. She tried to clear the fumes from her head by wondering what he'd done to earn the calluses; men who headed large businesses didn't usually have time—or the inclination—for vigorous manual exercise.

Hunt Radcliffe, it seemed, made his own rules.

Some elemental part of her brain manufactured an image of that strong hand against the fine-grained softness of her skin, the small roughnesses stimulating her nerves to painful intensity.

The silence seemed to whisper of forbidden hunger.

She swallowed and said in a muted voice, 'I believe New Zealand is very beautiful. I know Alexa misses it sometimes.'

'Loving Luka must make up for that.'

He had no idea how much his words hurt; loving Luka would, she thought wearily, make up for anything!

Cia hoped she hid her surprise. He didn't seem the sort of man who believed in love. In fact, a magazine had featured him as one of the most determined bachelors in the world. She remembered the parade of photographs that had accompanied the article—snaps of him with beauties of all types clinging to his arm.

'Of course,' she said without expression. 'Whereabouts in Northland do you live? Close to Auckland, I suppose.' It was logical that he'd live near the country's biggest city; he spent a lot of his time commuting around the planet.

'On a hill not far from a place called Doubtless Bay.' When he saw that she didn't recognise the name he added, 'In the far north.'

Visualising a map of New Zealand, Cia saw in her mind's eye the long, thin peninsula sticking up towards the tropics. 'Oh, a long way from Auckland.'

'About four hours' drive, or an hour's flight.'

'Not close,' she said, wondering why he'd sounded so abrupt. Had her throwaway suspicion of this morning perhaps been accurate—did he love Alexa?

She stole a glance up at him, secretly inspecting a profile etched against the soft glow the city lent to the sky. The harsh male combination of angles and lines summoned a heady rush of adrenalin. Something in him reminded her of Luka. Both were men born to rule.

If he did love Alexa, she thought sadly, he was too late, because his countrywoman truly loved her husband. It was there in her eyes every time she looked at Luka, in her smile, in her voice whenever she said his name. Nobody could mistake it.

# CHAPTER THREE

MORE lights bloomed in the pavilion behind them and voices rose above the calls of the tree frogs. Relieved, her emotions too close to the surface to be comfortable, Cia swung around and said, 'Ah, here's everyone else.'

To her surprise Hunt offered his arm. 'Those shoes aren't made for climbing steps,' he said when she glanced up.

Over the years she had rested her fingers on the arms of innumerable men, yet she hesitated a fraction of a second before accepting the unspoken invitation.

His teeth flashed white in the dusk. 'Scared, your highness?' he asked in a voice that sounded like the sort of purr a lion might produce.

Sarcastic jerk! Her hand trembled on his arm. 'Terrified,' she parried. 'As you've pointed out so graphically, a woman never knows what a man might be thinking.'

He laughed, deep and low and mocking. 'I'm thinking what every other man who gets this close to you does—that you're beautiful.'

Well, she'd handed him that opportunity on a platter. The only thing to do was treat it like a real compliment. 'Thank you,' she said with false cordiality. 'And you're very good-looking too.'

'Thank *you*.' But he hadn't finished. 'I'm also wondering if you ever let the real Lucia Bagaton emerge from behind the princess mask.'

Stung, she returned, 'How sad that you're never going to find out.'

Hunt's eyes gleamed in the soft light. 'Now there's a challenge,' he said softly.

She stiffened and began to step away, but when Luka and Alexa came out onto the steps, a lean tanned hand covered the pale one on his black sleeve. His touch—and the very narrow, very masculine smile accompanying it—sent tiny rivulets of fire rippling through her.

'I don't do challenges,' she retorted, nerves tightening as she met his eyes.

Hunt removed his hand. 'You challenge me every time you look at me. But don't worry—I'm past the age of taking dares just for the hell of it. Nowadays I need to know that there's something in it for me.'

That final remark sounded so much like a threat that Cia retorted with a crazy lack of caution, 'Spoken like a true tycoon!'

His cold glance caught hers, refused to let it go. 'So you don't need to worry, princess,' he said obliquely. 'I'm not going to climb the tower and claim any reward.'

But the ruthless note through the words shivered down her spine, dousing her inner fire with foreboding. She couldn't think of anything to say so she settled for nothing as they climbed the steps towards Alexa and Luka.

Much later, creaming off cosmetics in front of the mirror, Cia decided ruefully that the ancestor who'd enjoyed building follies would have been happy with the evening; it could have sprung straight from his imagination.

Beautiful women in elegant clothes and jewels flirted with handsome men—some even had interesting conversations. The whole event was permeated by the smell of privilege, embellished by superb food and magnificent wines and seasoned with laughter. The croaking of tree frogs provided a suitably exotic background for those not born on Dacia, and as a final offering, a huge, wine-red Mediterranean moon, fat with promise and mystery, had risen above the edge of the sea to drench them in magic.

Of course Hunt had fitted in; he was a man who'd cope brilliantly with any situation. Millionaires usually were, she thought snidely, lowering her lashes to remove the last trace of eye-shadow.

Every time she'd looked across he'd been either talking man to man, or indulging in sophisticated banter with a woman. Her sex made much of him, the unattached ones especially; she had overheard one invitation delivered with subtlety by a Frenchwoman renowned for her beauty and her discretion.

He'd refused it with a smile in which there had appeared no hint of the cynicism he'd used on her.

Not that it mattered! She didn't give a hoot what Hunt thought of her. As for the fact that he hadn't danced with her—well, she didn't care about that either.

Not a bit.

Someone knocked on her door. Hastily she wiped the last of the cleanser from her skin and went across to open it, tightening the belt of her robe around her narrow waist.

It was Luka. Anxiously she asked, 'What is it?'

He said, 'I'd hoped you hadn't changed yet. Can I come in?'

'I—yes, of course.' Frowning, she asked, 'Is anything wrong?'

'No.' He frowned. 'How long have you known me, Cia?'

'Since I was born,' she said promptly, wondering what on earth this was all about.

'First as a cousin, and then as a kind of substitute big brother and father.' He looked around her luxurious bedroom. 'I have been very unfair to you—keeping you chained here when you should have been out enjoying life and find-ing yourself.'

'I've enjoyed my life very much, thank you! And I never lost myself.'

Luka stood looking at her with an expression she couldn't read, then said abruptly, 'As one adult to another, I must tell you that although—*because!*—Hunt Radcliffe is an ex-citing and very sophisticated man, he is not a man to fall in love with.'

'Did Alexa suggest you talk to me about this?' she asked stiffly.

His face hardened. 'No. I saw immediately that he was interested in you—and why not? You are as beautiful as a spring day. I know we joked about him being attractive, but tonight it seemed to me that perhaps you are intrigued by him.'

Cia relaxed. 'I find him interesting,' she admitted, 'but I'm not silly. I can recognise a heartbreaker when I see one.'

'I wouldn't call him that,' Luka said fairly. 'His women so far have not been the type to put their hearts in jeopardy. But you're not like them. And he has a lot more depth to him than, say, young Lorraine. I love you, and I would hate to see you hurt, little sister.'

It was unbearably painful to hear him say that, when for years she'd longed for an entirely different sort of love from him!

'I won't be hurt,' she said briskly, and summoned a slant-ing smile. 'Anyway, he doesn't like me. I think you could probably say that we're polite antagonists.'

The prince looked wryly at her. 'Some men find it very difficult to deal with the women who break through their shields,' he said, his voice revealing that he knew what he was talking about. 'They have always considered them-selves to be strong and invincible. When they discover that one woman can shatter that belief, they—resent her.' He paused, then added with a smile that hurt her, 'For a while, anyway, until they admit that for them this is the only woman in the world.'

As Alexa was for him.

'Don't worry about me,' she said brightly. 'He's very attractive, but I meet attractive men every day. I'm not going to fall in love with him!'

He frowned at that, then said unexpectedly, 'Alexa tells me that I still think of you as the lost child who first came here. Perhaps I do.'

She had never loved him quite so much as she did that moment—and never wanted quite so hard to kick and scream and tell him that for an astute, intelligent man he could be extremely dim!

But she'd been so careful to hide her secret—how could she blame him for not noticing? Tears clogging her throat, she smiled mistily at him and said, 'Luka, you couldn't have been a kinder, more affectionate big brother. I hate to think how I would have grown up if I hadn't had you to believe in me and take care of me.'

Thoughts of her mother, dead too young from a drug overdose, of her charming, irresponsible father, hovered between them.

'You'd have managed,' he said confidently. 'You're a lot stronger than either of your parents—the Bagaton blood runs true in you. So—goodnight, then.' He dropped a kiss on her cheek and left the room.

The word that wept through her heart was goodbye. Goodbye to everything she loved, to her island home, to the man who'd made her life worthwhile.

Once the door closed behind him she sat down on the bed, looking around the room that had always been hers, at first during the school holidays, later permanently. Although

Luka's father, the old prince, had been kind enough, to him she was simply another responsibility.

Luka had filled the gap in her life; he had taken her skiing and corrected her swimming strokes, he'd taught her how to play chess and insisted she keep up her piano lessons. He'd loved her.

But not the way she wanted him to.

Slowly she got up and began to take off her robe. Leaving Dacia had been the right decision.

'Oh, admit it,' she said aloud into the silent room as she climbed into her pyjamas, 'you stayed on because you're a coward—because the thought of leaving hurt too much.' And because even the bittersweet pain of seeing Luka with Alexa was better than not being near him.

Now it was the staying that hurt too much. Cia's heart twisted; unless she could exorcise Luka, she'd be doomed to the life of good works Hunt had been so snide about.

Tears drowned her eyes. She sniffed and wiped them away with the back of her hand, but they kept coming so in the end she had to find a handkerchief.

How did you banish someone from your heart—from your life? She'd loved Luka since she was old enough to understand her own emotions.

So why, a strange voice inside her mind queried interestedly, do you shiver whenever Hunt Radcliffe touches you?

Jolted out of self-pity, Cia blew her nose with determination. Her violent response to Hunt was nothing more than an involuntary chemical reaction—neither her mind nor her emotions were involved.

It was humiliating that the real Cia, the person who lived in her head and found Hunt overbearing and arrogant and sarcastic, seemed to have no control over the body that smouldered into life when he touched her.

'It's embarrassing, but it's not fatal! It's not even important,' she muttered defensively, and finished getting ready for bed.

This brash, uncomplicated, sexual attraction was notoriously unreliable when it came to relationships. How many kings had lost their countries because they'd let themselves be carried away by passion?

'Too many to count,' she said sternly, switching off the light.

Of course she wasn't a king with a country to lose, but she'd seen enough of transient relationships to know they weren't for her. She wanted love and permanence, and judging by the gossip columnists, Hunt didn't stay faithful to a woman for more than a year or so.

She curled up in the big bed and stared out at the stars of Dacia. As her body relaxed she let her mind drift, only to shock herself by wondering whether giving in to this risky attraction—having an affair with Hunt—would finally exorcise Luka from her heart.

Smiling, she slipped into a heady fantasy where Hunt bent towards her with passion warming his midnight eyes, and she reached out and touched his beautiful mouth with trembling fingers while he murmured her name...

'No!' she exclaimed, sitting bolt upright in bed, utterly disgusted with herself for thinking about using another person, even one as arrogant as Hunt.

She'd already done that when she'd tried so hard to fall in love with Maxime. She'd liked him so much, had allowed herself to hope that their rapport was the beginning of love, only to find out she'd been completely and painfully wrong.

She wasn't going to do that again. Oh, Hunt was tough; he wouldn't look for love from her, and he certainly wouldn't be heartbroken when the affair ended, but she still couldn't do it.

She switched her light back on and picked up a book, reading with stubborn determination until she couldn't see the words on the page. Sleep claimed her like a devouring beast, but towards dawn her restless dreams were invaded by the man whose touch shortened her breath and set her heart pounding in an erotic rhythm.

In her dreams an unknown, bold Cia surrendered joyously to Hunt's touch, following recklessly where he led, her imagination supplying details of experiences she'd never had...

She woke in a dazed, blissful euphoria that rapidly diminished to hot shame. Let loose in sleep, her unconscious brain had shocked her with its explicit imagery.

In the misty light of dawn she knew that an affair with Hunt Radcliffe would be a quick path to disillusion. Sensual charisma swirled around him like a dark cloak, and he wouldn't be impressed with a lover whose experience was limited to Maxime's attempts to arouse her.

'Don't even think about it,' she adjured herself.

But a smouldering, heady anticipation infuriated her as she got out of bed.

Because Alexa and Luka both had appointments that morning she was to escort Hunt on a sightseeing tour. Her stomach tightened, and when she looked in the mirror she saw a gleam in her eyes and a wash of delicate colour along her cheekbones.

What kind of woman loved one man yet indulged in erotic fantasies about another?

'My kind, apparently,' she said grimly, and left her room.

Breakfast over, they came out of the doors of the Little Palace. Hunt looked at the chauffeur standing by the door of the car. His brows rose. 'Can't you drive?'

Cia bristled. 'Of course I can.'

'Are there security reasons that make a driver necessary?'

'Not on Dacia.'

His disciplined mouth curved into a hard smile. 'Do you feel safer with a chaperon?'

'No,' she snapped, temper flaring because somehow he'd hit the nail on the head—and she hadn't even realised what she was doing until he'd called her on it!

Reining in her unusual anger, she countermanded the order and asked for her own car to be brought around.

It amused her in an acid way to note that he watched her carefully for the first few minutes, yet she felt a swift glow of pride when he relaxed.

'You drive well,' he observed.

'Thank you. Luka taught me.'

He nodded without surprise and looked out, dark eyes sharply perceptive as she took the road up into the hills to the place where the first inhabitants of Dacia had lived. Amongst the rocks of the wall that sheltered the dark mouth of the cave, small, vivid cyclamen flowers nestled in mounds of silver-splotched leaves.

'I suppose there's a legend about this,' Hunt observed as they walked through a grove of myrtles to the entrance.

The high-pitched zither of cicadas strummed all about them, and the sun beat down on his proudly poised head, turning the mahogany highlights in his hair to fire.

He looked, Cia thought with an odd catch in her breath, like a statue newly forged as a symbol of male power and grace and beauty. A twisting, unexpected sensation arrowed down to the pit of her stomach.

'There's always a legend. The original Dacians believed their major god was born in the cave.' She swallowed an odd hoarseness to continue briskly, 'Once Christianity reached the island it became transformed into the dwelling of the hermit who is now the island's patron saint.'

He nodded. 'The usual progression.'

Cia must have shown her surprise, because his eyes glinted as he drawled, 'You've known Alexa for long enough to realise that coming from the Southern Hemisphere doesn't mean we're barely literate.'

'Most of the very rich men I've known,' she retaliated smoothly and not quite truthfully, 'are interested in very little more than making money or spending it. It's so refreshing to meet one who has a broader spread of conversational topics.'

He grinned. '*Touché!* I'm sure you feel happier now you've got that off your chest.'

Cia couldn't stop her reluctant smile as they walked around the end of the rock wall and towards the grille that barred the entrance of the cave. 'You're a maddening man,' she said. 'Does anyone ever get the better of you?'

'It happens.' He examined the padlocked door. 'Do we go inside?'

'I have a key.' She produced it from her bag.

When Hunt held out his hand she automatically gave the key to him, wondering as he opened the gate why she'd let him take over. Because he's a take-charge man, she thought. Like Luka. Setting her lips she began to walk into the darkness.

'I'll go first,' Hunt said.

She stopped. 'Why?'

'For some reason it goes against the grain to let a woman go into darkness ahead of me, so you'll have to surrender your royal prerogative just this once.'

Smarting at the jibe, yet oddly touched by his inherent sense of protectiveness, she said, 'There's nothing in there.'

'So why the grille? I wouldn't have thought you'd have much of a problem with vandals.'

'We don't. Most locals won't come anywhere near the place; the island's patron saint was not noted for his friendly temperament and he was a most determined hermit, so very few Dacians are prepared to cross him.'

Hunt set off into the dark mouth of the cave. 'In that case, why is the grille needed?'

Following him, she shrugged. 'It's a historically important site, and every so often someone—usually a tourist—decides they might find something exciting, like gold ornaments.'

The entranceway narrowed and turned abruptly away from the light. She said, 'Careful, there's another sharp turn—*oof*!'

Her last words were muffled as she collided with him. In the half-second before she leapt back she registered muscles like steel and a faint, intensely masculine scent that shivered through her like an aphrodisiac.

'I saw it,' he said drily. 'Are you all right?'

'I'm fine. You must have eyes like a cat,' she returned. 'There's a light sw—'

This time the words dried in her mouth. Wide eyes rapidly getting used to the darkness, she caught the white flash of his smile.

'Not yet.' Strong hands clamped onto her shoulders. 'Shall we get it over and done with?' he asked pleasantly.

Nerves jumping, Cia looked up into his dark face, suddenly predatory in the dim light. 'I have no idea what you're talking about,' she said with a brave attempt at her usual crispness.

'It's inevitable, and until it's happened you're going to walk around me as though I'm contagious.'

Her heart revved up, skipping beats in excited terror. 'I don't know what you mean,' she retorted breathlessly.

'This,' he said on a note of impatience, and bent his head and kissed her.

The warm, exploratory touch of his mouth against hers

surprised her with the sensuous pleasure it aroused. Once she realised he wasn't going to stick his tongue down her throat, she relaxed and kissed him back. Sharp and sexy, his natural scent echoed the man—a faint touch of salt, an edgy hint of musk—a fragrance that owed nothing to artificial means.

When he lifted his head Cia sighed silently with guilty, astonished pleasure, astonished to realise that somehow her hands had stolen around his neck and she was now pressed against him.

She could feel how much he liked it—and his obvious physical enjoyment at her closeness didn't repel her at all. Deep inside her something melted, hot and eager and ardent, both shy and avid.

'Nice,' he murmured, and kissed her again, a little less gently.

And then his mouth changed from warm and coaxing to a hard urgency that demanded infinitely more than she'd ever given any other man. An enormous, irresistible force swamped her in a tidal wave of sensation. She wanted him—she wanted everything he could give.

Here.

Now.

When his arms tightened around her, she shuddered with delight at the intensely intimate contact of her body with his big, powerful one. Hunt took instant advantage of her instinctive reaction, sending her excitement soaring to stratospheric heights as he explored her mouth with shattering expertise.

*So this is what all the fuss is about.*

Shocked by the violence of her hunger, she abandoned herself to the wave after heated wave of passion that clamoured through her. Her brain closed down and she surrendered wholly to the fiery, carnal possessiveness of his kiss.

Until he lifted his head and surveyed her flushed face. He couldn't hide the colour along his warrior's cheekbones or the dark glitter in his narrowed eyes, but his voice was cool and unsparing.

'There,' he said, 'now it's over and done with, you can stop peering at me every five minutes with that hunted expression.' His hands dropped and he stepped backwards.

Alone and cold, the primitive excitement that flooded her body draining away to leave her coldly disgusted with herself, Cia fought for control. Although she loved Luka, she was shaking with frustrated desire for this man—even now, if he touched her she'd follow him.

From somewhere deep inside, she summoned enough poise to say remotely, 'I'm sorry if I gave you that impression.'

'Why? In case you hadn't noticed, it's entirely mutual.'

Gritty pride tilted her chin and banished everything but brittle composure from her voice. 'I'm not hunting, Mr Radcliffe. There should be—ah, here it is.'

Although the last thing she wanted him to do was see her face, pride drove her to touch the switch. She used the sudden blare of light as an excuse to blink back meaningless tears while she stared blindly around at the rocky walls of the cave.

# CHAPTER FOUR

HUNT had only kissed her! But his kisses had rocked her world. Instinct warned Cia it would be dangerous to let him know that.

She glanced at his angular face, dark and forbidding in the light of the bulbs suspended from the ceiling of the cave. The hard lines and planes revealed nothing but interest in his surroundings. Thank God he didn't seem to be thinking about her reckless response.

Of course, an experienced lover like him probably expected that sort of unleashed reaction from any woman he kissed!

When Cia regained control over her vocal cords, she indicated the area that had been dug over by archaeologists. 'It's been a couple of years since any work was done here, and as you can see, there's nothing exciting about the site. Most of the artefacts are in the museum in the port, if you're interested.' Yes, that sounded fine—entirely normal.

Hunt looked down at her. 'Oh, I'm interested,' he said silkily.

Her reply dried on her tongue and she couldn't rescue her imprisoned gaze from his. Disjointed images scurried uselessly through her brain—the cold blue gleam of moonlight on a sword blade, a warrior in full battle array mounted on a screaming war horse, a silken, perfumed, decadent pavilion in some exotic country...

Hunt finally released her by turning to survey the site. 'Does it go any further into the hill?'

Plumbing the depths of her soul, she summoned more

pride to stiffen her spine and lend some authority to her voice. 'No. This is all there is.'

She walked across to the roped-off area where the archaeologists had worked and began to tell him—in her best tourist guide's tone—of the things they'd found.

He knew enough about archaeology methods and European prehistory to keep her alert; at any other time she'd have enjoyed discussing it with him. For now, concentrating helped restore vague order to the chaos that passed for her mind, and gave her something else to think about besides her body's meltdown.

Although dank, it wasn't cold inside the cave, but it was cooler than the warm spring day outside. Not, however, cool enough for the sudden shiver that shook her.

Hunt said instantly, 'Let's go.'

He took her elbow as they walked out along the rutted path. Cia's skin tightened in a primitive, violent response. Every time he touched her she was changing, growing more and more sensitive to his touch.

Where to now? Somewhere with people, she decided, even as her mind muttered, *Coward!*

Despising herself, she said brightly, 'Luka plans to show you his reforestation schemes later in the week, so would you like to see the Old Palace now?'

Hunt's satirical smile didn't soften his striking features. 'Why not?'

'The Old Palace started out as a Greek colony before being transformed into a Roman fortress,' Cia told him, easing out of the traffic to negotiate the breach her nineteenth-century ancestor had made in the massive walls. 'After the Romans fell it suffered the usual fate—everyone who wanted to control this part of the world fought their way in here and proceeded to claim tribute and oppress the islanders.'

Hunt eyed the huge stones. 'I can see why Alexa and the prince prefer the Little Palace,' he observed. 'This looks as though it's been literally drenched in blood—and not just once, either.'

'It was never overthrown after the first Bagaton prince moved in, but you're right, it's certainly not cosy,' she said with a faint smile, nodding to a saluting sentry. 'Luka's father was the last prince to actually live in it.'

'From what I've heard, he'd have suited it.'

'He was a hard man,' she returned coolly, 'but he lived in difficult times, and everything he did was for Dacia. Given the need, Luka can be hard too.' She paused, and added with a faint note of malice, 'And that, I understand, is your reputation as well.'

'Sprung.' Lazy amusement warmed his voice. 'So a certain amount of ruthlessness is fine if it's for your country, but not for personal gain? Somehow, princess, I think you've got me positioned as one of those rich men you despise.'

He was too damned astute, and although crossing swords with him was exhilarating, she had painted herself into a corner. She drove past the huge doors to pull up outside a small entry around the corner. 'Nonsense,' she said briefly, killing the engine. 'I don't know you well enough to make any judgement.'

He laughed, low and quiet. It was stupid to read something of a threat in his words when he said, 'I'm surprised and rather disappointed; I feel I know you quite well.'

Colour sizzled along her cheekbones. 'Only by reputation,' she said, unnerved. 'And I'm sure we're both too astute to rely on newspapers and paparazzi for information!'

If she had to drive Hunt again she'd order a bigger car. He took up far too much room—and not just physical space! He crowded her. And she couldn't prise the memories of his kisses out of her mind. They replayed in endless, sexy invitation.

Nailing a smile to her lips, she got out and headed for a small side entrance where an attendant waited. 'Hello, Paolo. Happy name day for next week.'

The young man beamed at her, a beam that faded when it collided with Hunt's sardonic blue gaze. 'Thank you, your highness.'

'How is your grandmother?'

'She is improving so much after you and the Princess Alexa visited her! My mother says it has given her a new lease of life.'

'Excellent!' Cia gestured towards Hunt. 'I'm going to show Mr Radcliffe around the palace.'

He gave a little bow. 'Do you want the rooms cleared of visitors, ma'am?'

'No, it won't be necessary.'

Hunt waited until they'd reached the audience chamber before enquiring thoughtfully, 'Do you know everyone on the island?'

'I've got a good memory for names and faces—probably bred in my bones!—and it's not as though the island has a huge population.'

He surveyed the great hall; the most determined efforts of nineteenth-century princes hadn't been able to transform the huge area. It was still a grim mediaeval space..

'This looks suspiciously like the real thing,' he observed drily.

Her ripple of laughter lightened his mood. 'I think my forebears realised they weren't going to be able to civilise this part of the palace so they just replaced what decayed and left it alone. Most of the banners are reproductions— over the centuries the original ones were eaten by various insects with exotic tastes.'

Hunt ignored a woman staring blatantly at them. 'Did you visit Dacia much before you came to live here?'

'My father didn't get on with Luka's and my mother hated the place, so we only came a couple of times. After their marriage broke up, Dacia wasn't on anyone's agenda.'

Hunt heard the reservation in her voice. No doubt she knew the sordid reality of her mother's death from a drug overdose; it had been splashed over all the tabloids. Not that Princess Lucia seemed to have suffered much angst from her unconventional upbringing.

Gaze fixed on one especially large banner, dimly colourful in rich, sombre tones, she finished, 'But after my father died I spent almost every school holiday here.'

A shaft of light from a high, narrow window struck her hair, shimmering blue fire across its sleek black crown. The curve of her cheek and long, elegant line of her neck and throat stirred his hormones into sudden, inconvenient activity. Kissing her had been a supremely stupid thing to do. He could still taste her, startled at first, then sweet and soft and fiery, her body sleek and eager against his.

She looked up, and colour bloomed along those incredible cheekbones, while her lips, a little more full than they'd been before he'd kissed her, tightened.

Retiring behind a wall of aloof formality, she took him conscientiously around the old fortress, telling him of old feuds and intrigues, tragedies and battles, with the vivid realism and black humour of someone who'd learned the tales from the inside.

Normally Hunt would have found it interesting, but today the primitive desire that smouldered through his body got in the way. He found himself listening to the cadences of her voice rather than the words, and watching her with an intensity that warned him not to touch her again.

Was that how it had begun with Maxime? Torrid, uncontrollable passion a first step to the lonely road that had finally led to a miserable death from fever in a foetid tropical jungle?

Hunt stared at a sword in the armoury.

'It's a mediaeval broadsword,' Cia told him, her voice wry. 'Luka the Third demolished an invading army with it.'

Hunt's brows lifted. The blade was huge, free of any ornamentation. 'It certainly looks as though it means business, but a whole army?'

Her amber eyes gleamed with shared amusement. 'He was an excellent ruler for his time—'

'Which means he was ruthless but with huge charisma.'

'And devious and cunning,' she added with a laugh. 'Fortunately he was also intelligent, so he knew the value of a good myth. When his people attributed the victory to him alone, he accepted it.'

Hunt scrutinised the blade. A stain of some sort—not rust—ran from the tip to halfway up the blade.

Beside him Cia said lightly, 'Another myth says that that's the bloodstain from a particularly cruel pirate who tried to take over Dacia.'

'And what do you say it is?'

She shrugged. 'Nobody's ever been able to work that out.'

They moved on to examine an elaborate suit of armour. The faint, flowery scent she wore floated upwards. Hunt took a deep breath. A surge of need so intense it felt like craving made him grit his teeth.

Lucia said blandly, 'The princes were great collectors; some of it's exquisite, but more than a little is high-class trash—and some that's just spectacular.'

Hunt regarded a stuffed bear holding a tray in its forepaws, then transferred his gaze to her. 'Spectacular is the only appropriate word,' he said ironically, something in his tone making Cia uneasy.

She risked a quick glance, and caught a fleeting hint of sexual awareness. It vanished immediately from his boldly chiselled features—if it had existed. She'd probably misread his expression.

In a cool, unemotional tone she said, 'I believe this particular stuffed bear was used to collect visiting cards. The crown jewels are much more interesting.'

And more private, she hoped. Several people had been following them around, hovering close by whenever they stopped.

If they were trying to overhear their conversation they'd be disappointed; Hunt was too accustomed to the need for discretion to make any comment that couldn't have been broadcast over the island television station.

The intrusive interest, she thought as they moved into the treasury, was one thing she wouldn't miss when she left Dacia.

Ten minutes later Hunt looked up from a heavily secured case that displayed several exquisite emerald tiaras. 'Which one do you wear?'

She shrugged. 'The smallest one, thank heavens—it's the lightest of the lot.'

He examined it, then scrutinised her sleek head until she shifted a little, her skin heating. Cold amusement glimmered in his eyes, but all he said was, 'How on earth do you keep it on?'

'The more hair you have to anchor it, the easier it is. The bigger one with the pearls is Alexa's, and the solid job with rubies as well as emeralds is the royal crown. My mother used to say that while all coloured stones were vulgar, two lots in clashing colours were positively barbaric, but she was an Englishwoman with refined tastes. Luka has the confidence to carry off anything.'

She was prattling because he hadn't taken his gaze off her, and little rills of sensation were shivering through her body. *Hot* little shivers, she thought in confusion, trying to censor this primitive, runaway response.

Eyes half-closed, Hunt said, 'Cognac diamonds would suit you better. Or would your mother have thought them vulgar too?'

Her colour deepened. 'Probably, but with so many emeralds lying around unused in the vaults no sensible ruler is going to waste money on other stones.' She finished with irony, 'Anyway, these aren't meant to *suit* anyone—they're meant to strike onlookers with awe and convince them they're in the presence of someone regal and impressive.'

'These magnificent gems would do that on their own. I've heard of the Dacian emeralds, of course, but I don't think I've ever been told where they come from and how they ended up here. It looks,' he said thoughtfully, leaning forward to examine a particularly fine stone set in a ring, 'as though someone plundered an entire emerald mine.'

Cia laughed. 'Something like that. One of my raffish seventeenth-century ancestors went adventuring in South America and bought his way back into his father's good graces with the sort of treasure trove you could only find in those days. Nobody ever discovered where he got it—or how. I think he was probably a pirate who stole them off a Spanish treasure ship.'

Hunt had a buccaneer's face, dark and dangerous and intelligent; mentally clothing him in seventeenth-century clothes, she could imagine him lethally swashbuckling his way across uncharted chunks of the map to fame and fortune.

'All in a good cause, as the prince's father used them to

found the Bank of Dacia, and the island's present prosperity,' Hunt said idly. 'It's a romantic story.'

Cia gazed at the brilliant gems, their deep green facets smouldering with a dark, almost certainly bloodstained, history. 'I think there was probably more gore than romance in the story. I can't take you into the vaults—as you can imagine, security is very tight—but if you're interested in the whole collection, Luka can show you.'

His broad shoulders lifted a fraction. 'Why not?' he drawled. 'I'd like to see what a king's ransom looks like, and I don't imagine any other graduate from the New Zealand social welfare system has paid a visit to Aladdin's Cave.'

How had he got from orphan to tycoon? By being very tough and very clever and a leader of men, she reminded herself. *And this is the man you thought you might have an affair with?*

Only if she wanted a severe case of scorched fingers.

'Why can't you go into the vaults?' he asked idly, stopping to examine the sceptre.

'The emeralds belong to Dacia, not me.' And just in case there was anything the least sinister in his question, she said, 'I'm the traditional poor relation.'

His brows lifted in ironic amusement. 'So I see,' he drawled, examining her with a connoisseur's appreciation of her designer clothes and immaculate make-up.

Little prickles stabbed her skin, were transmuted into a sharp excitement that strained every nerve. 'I have a clothes allowance,' she said tightly.

'And poverty is relative.'

She shrugged, regretting her impulsive remark. 'Indeed it is.'

From her mother's estate she received just enough to keep her from starving. Once away from the security net of her job and position in Dacia, she'd have to work, because after she'd finished university she wasn't going to accept any further money from Luka.

Apart from a further hitch of his brows Hunt made no comment, but on the way back to the Little Palace he observed, 'You're very good at showing visitors around. When you leave Dacia—if you ever do—you'd be a sitter for a job in the tourist industry. The high-end market, of course.'

Something about his deliberate tone lifted the hair on the back of her neck. 'As it happens, I am leaving,' she said calmly, turning off the crowded street to dive into a narrow alley with the aplomb of years of practice. 'But I won't be going into the tourist industry.'

There was a moment's silence. 'So what will you do?'

Cia braked swiftly, stopping behind a donkey doing its best to cause a traffic jam. 'Oh, I'll find something,' she said airily.

'Join the jet set?' Scorn laced the question.

Judgemental bastard! She curled her lip. 'Some of my best friends—even the occasional relative on my mother's side—are members of what you'd call the jet set.'

A vigorous altercation broke out around them, the flower-seller whose wares were being eaten by the donkey calling on all her saints to remove the animal to its natural home in Hades.

Hunt dropped a cool, sardonic remark into a sudden silence with devastating effect. 'You could marry well. It's a traditional career path for women in your situation.'

Cia said between her teeth, *'Impoverished princess newly out of a job but reasonably attractive seeks rich, aristocratic husband. Competent at organising social calendar and with suitable family contacts for any social climber?'* Her voice returned to normal. 'I don't think so.'

'Drop *aristocratic*,' he suggested cynically. 'Unless you can't conceive of marrying into the *nouveau riche*.'

Anger seethed inside her, but she responded cordially, 'If I were thinking of advertising in such a vulgar way, I probably would. I'm not a snob, and most aristocrats are finding things hard nowadays.'

'Oh, I'm sure you'd be far more subtle.' It was not a compliment.

She said between her teeth, 'As it happens, I'm going to university.'

'History of Art?' he suggested patronisingly.

'A BA,' she flung at him. 'At Oxford.'

The war outside broke out again in the sort of uproar only Dacians could produce. Lean fingers on the door handle, Hunt said, 'I'll see if I can help here.'

At that moment the donkey's owner managed to wrench the beast away from the flower-seller's blooms. It side-stepped and backed triumphantly into the car.

As the vehicle rocked, Cia commented, 'We don't have many donkeys now—most Dacians prefer motor scooters.'

'I can see why.' But he sounded amused rather than irritated.

'I like donkeys.'

This one was now braying with indignation; berating it severely and noisily, its owner finally managed to wedge it into a niche in the stone building.

Hunt observed, 'It seems that the antagonists in this interesting war of wills have just realised who you are.'

Apologising in rapid Dacian, the donkey's owner gazed around in despair before snatching a bouquet of freesias from the flower-seller.

Thrusting them through the window into Cia's face, he gabbled, 'So sorry, your highness. This spawn of the devil will be the death of me. You have no idea—'

'Not those, you fool!' the flower-seller snapped, deftly retrieving the freesias and replacing them with roses. 'Here, highness, roses to suit your beauty—and because roses are the flowers of love!'

She rolled magnificent black eyes at Hunt, who gave her a smile that made her laugh and fan her face with her hands.

With her lap full of scented roses, Cia said, 'Thank you, but—'

Hunt overrode her. 'You must let me pay for them,' he said easily.

'Ah, you must be our princess's countryman!' the flower-seller exclaimed in English, visibly impressed as she held out her hand for the money Hunt dropped into the palm. She leaned down to fix Cia with a bold gaze. 'Your highness, now that Prince Luka has taken himself a wife, isn't it time for you to find a husband? When are we going to see another royal wedding in Dacia?' Her shrewd black eyes roved from Cia's flushed face to Hunt's amused one.

Cia produced a smile. 'Unless Prince Guy has fallen in love, not for a while,' she said, then flushed as Hunt scooped the bunch of flowers from her lap. Their perfume swamped her, seductive, languorous as the smoky heat of summer, richly evocative.

His lean fingers lightly brushed her breast, sending sensation through her in a lightning assault that robbed her of her wits. Accident? It certainly appeared so.

The flower-seller laughed openly, straightening up and stepping back when Hunt turned and dropped the blooms into the back seat.

Still buzzing with a fierce, intoxicating undercurrent of arousal, Cia put the car into gear with a hand that shook too much for her comfort, waved to the small crowd that had gathered and took off too fast.

Hunt didn't say anything, although she knew he was smiling; keeping her profile stubbornly aligned at him, she debouched from the narrow maze of streets onto a wider road, grateful because the flow of traffic kept her concentrating.

She had not come out of that very well. Now rumours would be flying around the island—well, it didn't matter! By this time next week she'd have gone, without fanfare as she wanted, but for good.

Frowning into the sun, Hunt asked, 'What decided you to go to university?'

Had he picked up on her thoughts? Of course not.

'Because I want to.' She passed a truck and went on more crisply, 'I'm not necessary here any more. Alexa is already loved, but while I stay people will look to me instead of to her. They are used to me, you see. Once I go she'll take her rightful place in their lives.'

'So when is this?'

'Just after you leave.' She turned the car onto the road to the Little Palace.

He was staring straight ahead, heavy lids hiding his thoughts, but Cia had the uneasy sensation of wheels whirring in that clever, incisive brain.

Today had been a strain; tomorrow would be easier. Alexa had organised a yacht trip to an offshore island where they'd eat a barbecue lunch beside a lagoon famous for the lilies that bloomed around the silken stretch of water.

Cia looked around a beach so blazing white everyone—including the chefs at the barbecue—wore sunglasses. Another picture to warm a romantic's heart, she thought, aware of pain niggling at one temple. Men and women in designer beachwear stood or sat or swam, all chatting, all clearly having a very good time, while she seemed stuck under her own personal dark cloud.

At least with twenty people in close attendance she was

able to avoid Hunt; another restless night punctuated by luridly erotic dreams had convinced her to stay well away from him. His disturbing male magnetism was playing havoc with her sleep.

After making smiling progress along the sand, she sat down beside Alexa in the shade of the tamarisks, letting out a small sigh as the slightly cooler air caressed her hot cheeks.

'I love this place,' she said, averting her eyes from the beach. A few metres away, two gorgeous sisters in the latest bikinis were flirting with Hunt.

Alexa looked a little pale. 'So do I, although I didn't realise the scent of the lilies would be so heavy. They're not even in full bloom yet—it must be overwhelming when they're all out.'

'Is it too much for you?' Cia asked worriedly. 'We can leave—'

'And deprive Hunt of the sister act?' Alexa laughed. 'It might spoil his day. Anyway, you know we can't go. Not that I want to—I'm fine.'

'Shall I tell Luka?' Cia watched the oldest sister—by ten minutes—lift thickly curling lashes to Hunt with a pouting, provocative movement of her lips.

He gave her a wicked smile and said something that set both girls squealing with laughter.

'Don't you dare,' Alexa said swiftly, casting a smiling glance at the trio. 'I wonder what he said?'

'Who knows? He's obviously used to beautiful women,' Cia observed acidly.

'Well, yes.' Alexa sighed. 'Very rich men are, aren't they? It goes with the territory. The first time I saw Luka in the flesh, a truly stunning female was fawning all over him while she fed him oysters. He certainly seemed to be having a very good time.'

Cia forced a smile. 'But that was before he'd met you.'

The woman beside her gave a secret little smile as the prince strolled along and sat down beside her. Cia lowered her lashes; it seemed indecent to watch two people who smiled at each other like that. It's not fair, she cried in silent, bitter rebellion.

But then, who said life had to be fair?

Humiliation mixed in an intolerable fashion with a wholly unwarranted antipathy to the two girls who were flirting with Hunt.

Two men, she thought in disgust—how could she love one and shiver with debilitating anticipation when the other looked at her?

Away from both men, she might be able to sort herself out.

'I'll just make sure that everything's all right with the barbecue,' she improvised, and got to her feet.

That day set the tone for the rest of the week. Cia spent it torn by conflicting emotions, her grief at leaving Luka and Dacia somehow overshadowed by this reluctant, wildfire attraction to Hunt that seemed to grow exponentially every time she saw him.

Which wasn't often; he spent much of the time in meetings with Luka and the executives of the bank. The evenings were busy social affairs.

Some time during the middle of the week, Cia realised she was actively looking forward to seeing him at night, crossing swords with him, indulging in a subtle, edgy sort of conversation that combined flirtation and aggression.

He took care not to touch her again, for which she was supremely grateful, but she was acutely, uncomfortably, recklessly aware of him. Watching him wield that ruthless charm like a weapon, Cia wondered if her mindless surrender had satisfied that predatory instinct she sensed in him.

So, he could now claim he'd kissed a princess. Big deal; besides, she couldn't see him as a trophy hunter. He was too confident to need public validation, which meant the gossip columnists weren't going to hear about it, and it was impossible to imagine him swapping stories of conquests with friends.

But perhaps the orphan from New Zealand enjoyed the thought of kissing someone from minor royalty.

No, she thought. Not Hunt. Unlike poor Maxime Lorraine, he didn't pin his self-esteem to anyone's opinion of him.

Every year, when the gardens reached their spring glory, Luka held an informal garden party in the Little Palace grounds, followed by a private dinner and a concert in the Old Palace. It was Cia's last official event and she had expected to be wretchedly miserable at it.

Instead, as she had every time they'd been in the same area together, she was watching Hunt from beneath her lashes.

Having apparently dumped his minder, he stood talking to a superbly dressed woman in her mid-thirties, who was flirting discreetly with him from beneath the brim of her hat. Her magnificent outfit might be more suited to a race meeting, but it certainly made the most of her lush figure.

I am not jealous, Cia thought valiantly, colouring slightly as Hunt looked over the top of the woman's elegant hat and sent her a long, direct, unsmiling stare, before switching his gaze back to his companion.

Icy little thrills scudded down Cia's spine. Each time their eyes clashed, she felt that it reinforced some kind of link between them. Yet there was none. Shocked by her body's awareness, she bit her lip and looked away.

From beside her Alexa murmured, 'Notice that it's always experienced women he flirts with? He won't be leaving any broken hearts behind him.'

Cia smiled stiffly. 'A week isn't long enough to break your heart over someone, surely?'

'I suppose not.' But Alexa sounded doubtful. 'Are you looking forward to your freedom?'

'Mostly,' Cia said promptly, not exactly lying. She had reached the state where her love for Luka was like a nagging tooth; she desperately wanted it out, gone, banished so that it no longer hurt.

'And you're happy to stay in the London house?'

'Until university starts, yes.' Not after that; living with constant reminders of the past would hurt too much, so she'd be looking for a place of her own as soon as she settled.

She was grateful when Alexa said, 'Ah, afternoon tea is served,' and together with Luka they went into the huge marquee.

Much later that night, after the concert, Cia changed into a long, drifting cotton dress in her favourite shade of amber, enjoying the freedom to banish all underwear but her briefs. The garden party had only just been in time; already heat was beginning to strike the island. Soon, when summer aridity took over from spring's lush promise, Dacia would bake under a relentless sun. Holidaymakers would pour in to toast themselves on the white sand and swim in sea as blue as the sky, drink the island wine and make love.

And she wouldn't be there.

Neither would Hunt. An aching restlessness drove her, and as she slid her feet into sandals—without heels this time—and went out into the corridor she tried to convince herself that she'd be relieved when he left. He was altogether too everything. Too dominant, too hard, too formidable, too sexy, too intelligent, too rich—oh, there were a multitude of *toos* that fitted Hunt Radcliffe!

Too much man for her.

She was still smiling ironically when she opened the side door and walked out onto the terrace. It was a night for lovers, she thought wistfully; the moon had just risen, the golden globe slightly diminished from its fullness of the night Hunt arrived.

Less than a week ago! It seemed that she'd been watching him hungrily from the corner of her eye for a lifetime.

And soon he'd be gone, and she'd probably not see him for years, if ever. Just as well; she couldn't blame him for her confusion, but loving Luka yet wanting Hunt was nervous-breakdown territory, she thought, trying to be flippant in spite of the stupid, silent tears aching in her throat. She needed time to sort herself out.

Her sandals made no sound on the flagstones of the terrace. Weak tears gathered in her eyes and began to slip silently down her face. Hastily turning onto a grass path in the intense darkness beneath a row of clipped cypresses, she blinked and swallowed—and froze when she heard voices coming slowly towards her. Alexa and Luka.

Too raw to want to talk, she acted on impulse, stepping quickly and silently into the deep shade of the cypresses and stood breathless, eyes clenched shut, hoping that they'd say nothing as they passed her.

But Alexa was speaking, and her words carried too clearly on the still, warm air. '...tell Cia?' she asked, her voice worried.

'No,' Luka said instantly. 'She'll insist on staying here if you tell her.'

Breath stopping in her throat, Cia gritted her teeth, trying to block out his statement, refusing to consider its implications.

But above the roaring in her ears she heard Luka say in a voice she barely recognised, 'My heart, my dear one, my most beloved, why can't I find the words to tell you how much I love you?'

Alexa said something, and he laughed deep and slow, and then there was silence. After a long time Cia opened her eyes and saw one silhouette disentangle into two; hand in hand, they walked in the kind light of the moon up towards the palace.

Indeed, a night for lovers.

# CHAPTER FIVE

LONG after Luka and Alexa disappeared, Cia stood staring blindly into the stiff shadows of the cypresses until she was certain she was alone. It hurt to breathe. It even hurt to take that first stumbling step out of the darkness into the silver brightness of the silent moon. Like a wounded animal, she sought sanctuary as far away as she could get from the Little Palace.

Down through the garden she walked swiftly and mindlessly, Luka's words playing over and over again in her brain. *She'll insist on staying if you tell her...*

Tell her what?

It didn't matter; he wanted her gone.

Blind instinct brought her to the summer house. Without turning on any lights she crossed the dining area and walked down the steps, made her way across the terrace to stop at the balustrade. Tree frogs croaked mournfully in the olive trees, and the scent of flowers hung like heavy smoke. Across the shadowy coastal plain by the port, someone was letting off fireworks.

Shivering in the warm evening air, Cia hugged herself and watched skyrockets soar into the dark sky. Each explosion into showers of glittering flowers hurt in some obscure way, yet she kept her gritty eyes fixed on each fresh golden arrow until the drifting sparks blurred and faded into nothingness.

Like stars snuffed out in the cold emptiness of space...

If only her emotions could end up as dark and dead as

the skyrockets, she might attain some peace. Unconsciously one hand went up to the pendant around her throat.

With a swift, fierce movement she whipped the chain over her head and clenched her fingers around the diamond star. Its sharp points cut into her palm. Pain and humiliation fuelled the impulse to hurl it over the balustrade. She even lifted her hand.

In the end she couldn't. Luka had given it to her with love; not the kind of love she craved from him, but love nevertheless. She couldn't throw it away.

When Luka had said, 'My heart, my dear one, my beloved,' each word had slashed through her heart like a sword, but now she knew it was time to relinquish the last, forlorn shred of hope.

But oh, it hurt so much…

She slid the pendant into her pocket and stared silently out over the plain as more skyrockets bloomed in the dark sky. She'd never wear Luka's star again.

Cia had no idea how long she stood there, dry-eyed yet aching as though she'd been physically beaten, but eventually she straightened up and dragged in a long, jagged breath. Wallowing in grief was not going to change anything. Life had to be lived, and the sooner she started, the sooner she'd be able to cope.

She swallowed the lump in her throat, then stiffened, hands gripping the balustrade. With renewed determination came something else—heightened perception that lifted the tiny hairs on the back of her neck. A panicky jolt under her ribs told her what the odd sensation between her shoulder blades had been trying to indicate for some minutes past. She wasn't alone.

One of the night-security men?

No, she thought, and slowly turned.

A tall dark shadow detached from the deeper darkness

inside the summer house, threading between the furniture with a powerful, lithe grace she recognised immediately.

'Hello, Hunt. Can't you sleep?'

'It must be the moon,' he said sardonically. 'What's your excuse?'

She sketched a brief, mirthless smile. 'Oh, I'll blame the moon too.'

Hunt stopped a pace away to look down at her, his striking face stripped to its essential strength by the hard white light of the moon. Cia's mouth dried; the elemental fire that burned in him banished her bleak chill in a surge of sensual heat. She felt dislocated, overwhelmed, her emotions jerked so swiftly from one extreme to the other that she was lost.

'The ancient Greeks had it right,' he observed, a raw edge to the words sending her heartbeat skipping. 'Their moon goddess was a chaste huntress, beautiful yet dangerous, and any man who saw her died.'

'She's long dead herself, poor Diana. You're the only hunter around tonight,' Cia countered, excitement binding her in molten chains.

'Am I?'

'My name isn't Diana,' she said unevenly. 'Lucia means light, not the moon.'

'But you're dangerous.' His smile, a masterpiece of irony, didn't quite hide the deep, abrasive note in his voice.

Every tiny hair on Cia's skin stood straight in sensual anticipation. From that first meeting this fiery anticipation had been building, building, building, until now it burned through restraint and reserve to fan her hunger into an inferno.

His smile hardened, but when she took a step towards him, tossing caution to that dangerous goddess of the night, he caught her by the wrist and held her away, scanning her face with dark intensity. 'What do you want, Lucia?'

For a moment she hesitated, torn between primitive longing and a valiant caution. Making love to Hunt would be using him...

But he wouldn't be hurt. He didn't even like her much, so it would mean nothing to him beyond easing his lust.

And oh, God, she needed warmth...

'You,' she said, the word whispering beneath the tree frogs' chorus. She wanted Hunt every bit as much as he wanted her—for different reasons, but he wasn't interested in her reasons.

'Your pulse is racing,' he said, his voice gravely neutral.

'I know.' She steepled the fingers of the hand he was holding so that she could rest the tips against his wrist. Touching him, feeling the slow regular beat begin to increase speed, gave her the same forbidden thrill as kissing him.

'So is yours,' she said on a ragged note.

'Why tonight?'

She glanced up, freezing as she braced herself for yet another rejection. But the bold features were clamped under such grim control she couldn't read his expression. In the moonlight his eyes glittered bright as diamonds, keen as the edge on a freshly honed blade.

She said briefly, 'Because it's a beautiful night.'

His mouth twisted and his voice was uncompromising. 'Tell me the truth.'

So she told him the truth—or as much of it as she was prepared to admit. 'It seems right. I want you, and I think you want me.'

After a nerve-racking silence he drawled, 'I didn't think you'd noticed, princess.'

'I'm going to stop you calling me that if it's the last thing I do,' she said between her teeth, and stepped into his arms and reached up, linking her arms around his neck.

And then her courage failed her.

His hands came up on either side of her head, holding her head still. For long moments he looked down into her questioning eyes, then lowered his head until his mouth touched hers in a kiss so gentle it seared through Cia like a laser.

She wanted heat and power and passion reckless enough to drive every thought from her brain, but Hunt gave her a cruel tenderness, exploring her face with his kisses until she groaned in supplication.

Then he laughed deep in his throat and swept her up, carrying her easily across to the biggest lounger. But before he put her down on it he asked, 'Is anyone likely to come here?'

Above the rapid, high thud of her heart she said, 'No, it's a private space.' And shivered in the crackling heat of the bridges she'd just set afire.

'I was thinking of your cousin.'

'No,' she said quietly. 'They've gone to bed for the night.'

Her voice didn't even tremble. Pain whispered below the surface, but held so close to Hunt, his faint scent mingling with the sultry perfume of the flowers, she couldn't feel anything other than urgent, primal anticipation.

'Good,' he said, the word echoing in her ears.

Still with her in his arms, he bent his head and kissed her again, and although he began with that intoxicating, dangerous tenderness, his mouth soon betrayed the urgency and raw force she needed so desperately.

Her lips softened beneath his, accepting and returning the wild heat of his kisses, so that when he at last put her on her feet she leaned against him and tried to regulate her breathing while she listened to his heart thudding in his chest.

'How does this pretty thing undo?' he asked, his amused tone not hiding the abrasive note in his deep voice.

'It doesn't.' She was nervous, but thank heavens for the training that kept her words level. 'It flips over my head.'

Expectation keen as a sword, she waited for him to strip her, but instead he kissed her again, and somehow when the kiss was over she was lying on the lounger with him—still with her clothes on.

Hunt slid an arm under her head and looked down into her face, his own cynically amused—and oddly determined. 'The moment I saw you I knew this week was going to be difficult,' he murmured, 'but it's been bloody murder. Since I lost my head and kissed you in the cave you've kept as far from me as you could, and every time I came anywhere near you, you gave me your princess smile, kind and interested and aloof. Each time I wanted to kiss that smile off your lovely face.'

Stung by his manifest unfairness, she said indignantly, 'You never came near me! You just looked at me occasionally—and you didn't smile at all.'

'Mm,' he said, kissing the corner of her mouth. 'I couldn't—I was too busy wondering if you tasted as good as I remembered…'

Hard and passionate, his mouth crushed the last sensible thought in her brain and carried her into the heart of a sun, burning away everything in a burst of need as powerful as a nova in explosion.

When he lifted his head she thought he said something against her lips, but she was too dazed to understand, and anyway, he kissed her again immediately and sweet, tantalising sensation flooded everything out of her mind. Sighing, she gave herself up to everything he demanded of her, shivering when his mouth explored pleasure points she dimly recalled reading about.

But no hearsay could have prepared her for Hunt's love-making. When he covered the throbbing pulse at the base of her throat with his mouth, it sent shudders of delight through her body, and when he nipped the lobe of her ear she almost cried out.

'Lucia,' he said deeply, and cupped her breast beneath the thin covering of lawn.

Her body tightened in delicious expectancy, arrows of pleasure shooting through her. Somewhere, she remembered, she'd read that men did what they wanted done to them, so she put her hand up and slid it through the buttons of his shirt. His skin was hot, and the soft friction of chest hair set her fingertips tingling and her heart banging against her ribs.

She looked up into smouldering, heavy-lidded eyes and saw him smile, a slow, wolfish movement of his lips that made her stomach kick in delicious panic.

'You can take it off,' he suggested.

With shaking fingers she undid the buttons and spread the thin cotton back to feast her stunned eyes on the magnificence of his torso.

He moved slightly as though she'd embarrassed him. Cia's breath sighed through her lips, and he laughed softly.

With shaking fingers she smoothed over the swell of one broad shoulder, simply enjoying the heated texture of his skin, fine-grained and flexible, beneath her palm. Hunt lay still, apparently happy to let her explore for as long as she wanted.

With renewed confidence, she remembered the exquisite pleasure of his hand against her breast; greatly daring, she progressed down towards a small dark nipple. He wasn't breathing, she realised with a sudden flare of fierce delight; this gave her the confidence to bend her head and kiss the tight, hard nubbin.

The big body beneath her lips jerked. 'Do you know what you're doing?'

She looked up, met gleaming eyes and a face set in taut, formidable lines.

'Do you like it?' she breathed, and lifted her head to trace a line of kisses across the swell of one roped muscle. It flexed beneath her lips, and she licked delicately, absorbing the salty taste of him, the clean male flavour.

'I like it.' Three guttural words, but they smashed through the last of her inhibitions.

Hunt reached up and with hands a little less deft than usual began to take the clips out of her hair. 'I've been having erotic dreams,' he said, a taut note charging his dark voice, 'of lying with your hair brushing against my skin like a cloak of silk. Trust me?'

Cia stared into eyes that were hard and hot as molten ebony. She didn't know what he wanted from her, but it was more than simple trust.

When she hesitated his eyes narrowed into fierce slits of steel. 'Don't tease the animal—it might bite. Say what you feel.'

For some reason she did trust him. She'd never have got this far if she hadn't been sure in some secret part of her mind that he wouldn't hurt her. When she nodded, the tumbling fall of her hair brushed against his skin.

'Yes.' The word fell on a soft, slumbrous cadence into silence.

He gave a low, clipped laugh and shrugged his shirt completely off his shoulders before lying back onto the lounger and examining her face, his eyes half-hidden by thick lashes. 'Just yes?'

'That's how I feel,' she said. 'One big yes.'

'Fortunately, that's exactly how I feel too.' He pulled her

down and slowly measured the length of her throat with kisses.

His skilful touch set free the wildness she'd tried so hard to contain. Bending her head, she explored his lean, powerful torso with eager mouth and questing hands, familiarising herself with his broad shoulders and rock-hard ribcage. Fascinated by the sheer male power beneath his sleek skin, the iron-hard muscles that coiled whenever he moved, she relished an odd, incongruous sense of being protected.

At last he said, 'My turn now.'

When Cia looked up, unnerved by his harsh tone, he slid her dress the length of her legs in an absorbed, intensely provocative movement, stroking skin silvered by the moon as the material moved up to reveal her legs. Sensation ran riot through her, melting her bones, pooling in her breasts and in the sensitive part between her legs.

Her breath locked in her throat; watching the lean dark hands against her skin, she had to force herself to drag air into her starving lungs.

When she swallowed, he said, 'Still yes?'

'Yes.' It was barely a sound. Everything had stopped, balanced on a knife-edge of anticipation; the owls no longer called, the tree frogs had fallen silent.

Slowly—*excruciatingly* slowly—he drew the soft thin fabric over her head. She lifted her arms and he pushed the material free of her, but instead of letting her go he held her wrists together above her head. Naked except for the narrow scrap of silk that hid her most secret parts, she felt her skin tighten, and her stomach contracted sharply as he scrutinised her body with leisurely thoroughness. Could he see her heart beating like a frenzied jungle drum? Did he understand that her breasts, soft and full and heavy, were waiting for something they'd never known...?

'I suspect that I'm going to end up like others who saw

the moon goddess,' he said deeply, moving to cradle her breast in his free hand.

The drum in her chest took over her body so that it throbbed with longing. She could feel the touch of those long fingers right down to the marrow in her bones, burning away everything but the need to experience Hunt in the most basic, intense way.

Her mouth was so dry she had to swallow hard before she could croak, 'Dead? I hope not.'

'There are different ways to die,' he murmured enigmatically, and pulled her towards him so that he could take the sensitive tip of her breast in his ravenous mouth.

This time she did cry out, transfixed by sensual pleasure so outrageously intoxicating she knew she'd never forget it.

Later, when her dazed mind went over the events of that night, she decided that Hunt was a devilish torturer—and oh, so experienced. By slow increments he led her further and further down the path of total abandonment, dazzling her with sensuous skill while he taught her eager body to accept every touch, every caress, every exquisite new sensation until, panting and desperate, she twisted in his arms, her hips rising instinctively against his big, potent body.

By then they were both naked. One long finger explored her most intimate parts; as she writhed against the voluptuous intrusion, he smiled and said softly, 'You're ready.'

She flashed, 'I've been ready for ages.'

'So it's mutual.' Smiling, he eased over her, and took her.

Cia had expected pain, but either riding horses or Hunt's meticulous preparation must have taken care of that, because he met no obstruction as he eased into her tight, slick passage. Ignoring a slight burning, a feeling of being forced to accept more of him than she had room for, she gasped, and once again her hips jerked upwards in unconscious invitation.

His face dark and intent and angular in the radiant light of the moon, he thrust home.

Her gasp turned into a kind of strangled groan, but she was beyond trying to analyse anything. A flood of strange, rich pleasure overwhelmed her, transforming her into a different woman, a woman who knew at last what her body had been made for.

Almost immediately, after a breathless moment during which her body began to adjust to the dominance of his, Hunt withdrew.

Instinctively she clung tightly, her fingers digging into his sweat-damp shoulders, and clamped her thighs together while she contracted muscles she didn't know she had, determined to keep him where he belonged, buried inside her.

He laughed deeply and lifted his hips, and she groaned again as he thrust deep, deep inside her, then withdrew again, setting up a rhythm that sent sensations bursting through her to destroy her final links to sanity.

She arched, pushing against his strength, those amazing inner muscles clamping onto him and relaxing in time with his movements.

With gritted teeth he muttered, 'No.'

Bewildered, she stared into narrowed eyes like molten ebony. 'What?'

'Next time,' he promised, each word thick and raw, 'you can do that and I'll hold out as long as I can, but right now this is going to come to an untimely end if you keep on doing that. Let's go gently.'

And that was wonderful too, until in the end the white-hot hunger inside her turned into waves that tossed her further and further towards a place she desperately longed to reach, but couldn't quite...

Hunt moved harder and faster, and she moved with him, their bodies dancing in an age-old pattern of desire and connection and offering until she convulsed in a cosmic inner explosion that flung her into an ecstasy so fantastic she thought she might die. Delight stormed her, took her prisoner, made her its own, and hurled her into a darkness where the only reality was Hunt and the response of her body to his.

Almost immediately Hunt made a deep, harsh sound in his throat. She forced up heavy eyelids to see him fling his head back.

As wonderful as her own climax was, seeing Hunt reach his drove her further up the heights of rapture until she cried out because she could bear it no longer.

And then it was receding and she was desperately trying to claw it back. Emptiness washed over her in a cold wave until Hunt's arms contracted around her, banishing that frightening sense of loss, and for the first time in her life she knew what it was like to be utterly secure.

'It's all right,' he said, kissing her forehead before smoothing back her hair. 'I'd like to lie here all night with you like this, but I suppose we can't.'

'No, it wouldn't be sensible,' she muttered, shocked by the sweet delight of this shivery aftermath, how easy it was to accept the warmth of his big body and to lie without strength against a heart that was still pounding like a piston.

He smiled, and ran his hand from her throat to her breast, smoothing the fine, damp skin in a caress that held tenderness as well as passion.

'And if we stay here for much longer,' he said, 'we're going to fall asleep. But we need to talk. Where are you going when you leave Dacia?'

'To the London house,' she told him.

He was silent for a short period. Cia didn't lift her head to look at him; it wasn't hope that struggled inside her. What they'd just shared was good sex—fantastic sex! How many women came to a climax like that the first time they made love? It was Hunt's expertise and astonishing tenderness that had done that for her, but she wasn't going to fall into the trap of thinking that sex was love—or even affection.

'Give me the address,' he said abruptly. 'I could meet you in London.'

Temptation knocked seductively on the door of her heart. He wasn't offering permanence, just a fling for a few days.

When he bent and kissed her, she shivered at the swift upsurge of desire. 'That's not fair,' she protested. 'I can't think when you do that.'

'That was the idea,' he said casually. 'You've got a couple of days to make up your mind. But just so that you don't forget—' he bent his head and girdled her waist with swift, hard kisses, taught her that her navel was another tiny erogenous zone, and then finished with a final kiss between her brows.

'Stop frowning,' he said against her skin. 'Meeting me in London is not such a big deal.'

'You can't control me with sex,' she said, although her voice wobbled.

He laughed. 'Why don't you try controlling me?' He glanced at his watch and swore under his breath. 'It's late, and tomorrow is going to be a busy day. Your cousin and I still have to hammer out the final details of our agreement. I believe we're having a quiet dinner tomorrow night.'

'Yes.' On impulse, she reached up and kissed his cheek, stimulated again by the soft abrasion of his beard beneath his skin.

'Not here at the summer house, I hope,' he said, irony hardening his voice.

Shivering, she sat up abruptly. 'No, not here.'

Hunt pulled her with him as he got up from the lounger

and tilted her chin with his thumbs so that he could see her face. 'Meet me in London,' he said quietly.

He didn't intend anything serious. For some reason that hurt, but she had to be sensible—making love to him could be addictive. However, a few wild days in London…

'All right,' she said.

His eyes gleamed in his dark face and he gave her a swift, hard kiss before letting her go. 'We'd better move.'

Cia felt awkward pulling on her dress and pants, but Hunt seemed perfectly at ease.

Naturally, she thought as she climbed into her sandals and recalled the sophisticated women he'd escorted; he was accustomed to this sort of thing.

It wasn't until she was showering back at the palace that she realised that making love to him had certainly done one thing for her—instead of breaking her heart over Luka's rejection, she was looking forward to going to London.

Which meant that her plan had worked; she had taken the first step to exorcising Luka from her heart.

She dismissed a pang of unease; OK, she'd used Hunt, but she had given him what he wanted. She was surprised that a man of his experience hadn't realised she was a virgin, but perhaps she was a better faker than she'd thought.

Now that he was coming to London, she'd have to make an appointment with the doctor. He'd used protection and she'd just had her period, so she was safe from pregnancy, but she needed back-up. She shivered, thinking of nights and days together in England.

Later, as pleasant exhaustion carried her towards sleep amidst the memories of what it had felt like to take him into her, she recalled that she'd once decided he'd make a bad enemy.

# CHAPTER SIX

WHEN Cia decided to leave Dacia she'd filled her diary with appointments, leaving free only the day before her departure. Thanks to the Hunt Radcliffe effect, she thought wryly as she got ready for dinner that night, she'd spent her last busy day in a suspicious glow instead of a haze of self-pity.

As for last night—well, that morning she'd woken in a panic, wondering what on earth she'd let herself do, but she'd calmed down during the day.

Whatever the outcome, Hunt had got her through a week she'd been dreading. For that she'd always be grateful. His presence on Dacia had made her life more sharp and vivid, more challenging.

In London that rich expectation would be amply indulged, but for tonight she'd let its slow simmer wrap her in its protective cloak. Mouth curving in an ambiguous smile, she settled the waistband of her pair of velvet trousers into place, and slid into a camisole top in matching topaz silk. The sensuous textures stroked her body, setting it purring. She pressed her hands to her hot cheeks, then snatched up the brush to control the wild confusion of her hair.

This satisfaction, the general well-being of a woman who had been well and truly pleasured—to use a nice old-fashioned term—wasn't happiness, but it was the only armour she had against the pain of leaving Dacia and Luka.

And Alexa. In spite of everything she had learned to love Luka's wife.

The brush slid through her hair in slow, even strokes and

she gazed into a misty distance, snatches of the preceding night playing through her mind.

If this was physical gratification, she thought dreamily, she was glad she'd experienced it.

That was when she caught a glimpse of golden eyes, satisfied and smug as those of a well-fed cat. Hot-cheeked, she focused sharply on her reflection. Unhappiness she could conceal; her sultry expression of anticipation and secret knowledge was a dead giveaway.

'Unless you want to proclaim to the world what happened last night you'd better get that look off your face,' she told herself, and began to ruthlessly pin up her hair.

On the way to Luka and Alexa's private apartment she wondered if Hunt was feeling anything like this languorous afterglow. But then, for him any morning-after-the-night-before satisfaction would be no novelty. And why did that thought sting like a poisoned dart?

She lengthened her stride. Grow up, she commanded. Jumping from the frying pan into the fire was not a viable life plan; she wasn't going to expect anything from a man who wanted nothing more from her than her body.

Her mouth firmed. Because that was all she would get from him—his splendid body, his skill as a lover, and the exciting aura that surrounded him. Hoping for anything else was asking for trouble.

When she walked into the drawing room, the expression on Hunt's strong-boned face didn't alter, although a smile of lazy appreciation glimmered in the blue depths of his eyes when he said her name.

A piercing stab of pleasure took her by surprise. Trying to ignore it, she shored up her self-possession and embarked on a round of small talk.

With no guests it should have been a pleasant evening, free from any strain. Hunt and Luka had come to an agreement that suited them both and both men were relaxed, clearly on the way to becoming friends. Alexa was her usual bright self.

Cia did her best, but tension slowly tightened her already overstrung nerves. After dinner she would have liked to excuse herself, but Alexa looked a little tired so she stayed, listening—and taking part in—the men's wide-ranging discussion.

Would Hunt try to see her alone before he left? Her heartbeat quickened at the prospect of days—and nights—with him in London.

Some time later she looked across the room and was astonished to see that Alexa had dropped off to sleep in the most charmingly natural way, her lovely face peaceful as her head tipped sideways in her chair.

The two men were talking about some complicated business scandal, so Cia got to her feet and said quietly, 'Alexa, would you like some coffee?'

Both men fell silent when Alexa woke with a slight start and gazed around, blinking several times.

'Coffee? No, thank you,' she said with a grimace, and then laughed a little. 'Oh, dear! How shaming!'

Luka came across and helped her to her feet. 'Bed,' he said calmly. 'I'll carry you.'

'I can walk.' She looked past him to Cia and Hunt. 'Sorry,' she said simply. 'I'm pregnant, and for some reason I keep going to sleep every time I sit down.'

Pregnant? Stabbed by unbearable, shameful envy, Cia's head swam and her heart contracted in acute pain. Desperately conscious that she couldn't let them see her face, she swung around.

Above the roaring in her ears, she heard Luka's quick, concerned voice. 'Cia—what is it?'

'Nothing.' Her voice came out as a harsh whisper, so she said again, 'Nothing! I was just—'

Hunt's saturnine features came into abrupt focus. She looked imploringly at him as the last remnant of her composure shattered into splinters.

Scarcely knowing what she said, she blurted, 'I can't leave Dacia now.'

Hunt's eyes gleamed cold and hard as quartz pebbles. He looked across her head and said smoothly, 'I've asked Lucia to come to New Zealand for a holiday, but if you need her to stay, Alexa, we can postpone it until you're feeling better.'

Stunned, Cia clamped her jaws together, but she seized on his words. Trust his cold, clever brain to come up with the one thing that would ease Luka and Alexa's mind. She'd almost given herself away so she had no choice. She had to fall in with Hunt's suggestion.

Making a good effort at concealing her surprise, Alexa said briskly, 'I'm perfectly all right—pregnancy is not an illness, you know. Luka, tell Cia she's not to waste the chance of a visit to Hunt's station!'

Cold emptiness beneath her ribs, Cia darted a glance at her cousin's stern face. Part of her longed for him to insist she stay.

Of course he didn't. After a slight pause he said, 'You must do whatever you want to, Cia, but Alexa won't need you to wait on her; the doctor says this tiredness is likely to pass when she reaches the end of the first trimester.'

Cia couldn't help saying, 'I feel as though I'm abandoning you.'

'Rubbish! We're going to miss you like crazy, but you've given up enough of your life for us,' Alexa told her seriously.

That was when Cia realised that this was what she'd overheard the previous night. They must have been talking of Alexa's pregnancy; they didn't want her on Dacia. Smiling steadily, she said, 'Then I'll go, but you must promise to let me know if you need me.'

'Of course,' Luka said, his voice giving nothing away.

He bent and picked up his wife, holding her as though she was the most precious thing in his life—as she was. Luka owed Dacia his duty, but Alexa held his heart.

Cia watched the other two leave, and felt Hunt's presence behind her.

Both were silent until the door closed behind them, when Hunt said in a flat, expressionless tone, 'You might as well come with me tomorrow.'

'I thought you were going to London?' Waves of reaction stripped her strength; she wanted nothing more than to collapse in a soggy heap on the sofa, but she forced herself to stand very straight, to meet his opaque eyes and huddle the tattered shreds of her composure around her.

He drawled, 'Only because *you* were planning to go there. Do you have appointments tomorrow?'

'I—no.' She swallowed.

'I'm leaving at eleven in the morning. Can you be ready by then?' No sign of the previous night's lover—he'd reverted to type.

The arrogant alpha male, she thought bleakly.

For years she'd managed to keep her emotions under control, ignoring her knowledge of Luka's lovers with stubborn fortitude. She'd even smiled like a pro throughout his wedding, yet one night in Hunt's arms had shredded her nerves so badly she'd almost tipped over the edge. If Alexa hadn't realised before, she certainly did now—and so, she thought sickly, might Luka.

What about Hunt?

He said, 'I'm sorry it got dumped on you like this. You've

done a magnificent job here and it's understandable you'd feel supplanted when someone else comes in to take your place. Alexa's been worrying—and worrying too that the baby will push you further into the background.'

Sheer astonishment kept her silent. Did he think she was so shallow that she—?

More gently, he went on, 'She won't feel so bad if she thinks you might be trying out your own wings.'

Cia glanced down at her hands, still rigidly held at her sides. So that was it; he was doing this for Alexa.

But not last night. Last night he'd wanted her, not Alexa. She should tell him the truth, and knew she couldn't. What would he think of a woman who made love to him when she was in love with another man? Thoughts ricocheted around her brain.

Finally she said, 'I don't think going to New Zealand would be a good idea.'

He smiled at her, and the sexual tension he'd unleashed the night before exploded through her bloodstream like some acutely dangerous designer drug.

'London, New Zealand, what's the difference?' he murmured, dropping a kiss on her mouth.

Cia swayed into his arms, and as the kiss deepened her hold on reality slipped. Hunt's touch submerged the shambles of her thoughts in a driving, desperate need.

After a frustratingly short interval he broke off the kiss and set her away from him, scanning her face with a possessive keenness that took no prisoners. His narrowed, glittering scrutiny almost branded her.

Hunt saw her hesitation. Her lovely face was expressionless; last night her collected poise had shattered in his arms, but she'd rebuilt it pretty damned fast.

If he hadn't seen that moment of desperation when she'd

realised that Alexa was pregnant, he might be thinking now that the news meant nothing to her.

The pity that had knotted his gut when he'd seen her reaction to Alexa's announcement intensified. He'd had to fight to make his position in the world and she'd been born to hers, but he could imagine his own reluctance to give up everything and sink into mediocrity. A couple of weeks in New Zealand would at least give her a break.

Then her head came up and she said with the remote aloofness that irritated the hell out of him, 'All right, I'll be ready tomorrow at eleven.'

He watched her leave the room and stood for a moment gazing down at hands balled into fists. Forcibly he relaxed them, looking up as Luka came into the room.

Cia made it, but only just.

That morning when she'd gone to say goodbye to Alexa, who'd decided to stay at home instead of going to the airport to see her off, Luka had demanded, 'Are you sure you know what you are doing?'

'Absolutely sure.' Pain twisted her heart as she went on doggedly, 'I'm having a pleasant holiday in a country I've always wanted to visit.'

'And you'll love it,' Alexa said, cutting off her last chance of retreat. 'Thank you for everything you've done for me and for Luka. You've been wonderful. And when you come back, come back with a happy heart.'

She knew.

'I will,' Cia said with a quick, awkward gulp, too emotionally spent to hide behind the mask she'd manufactured over the long years of loving Luka. She hugged Alexa back before pasting a smile onto her lips. 'Luka, the Victorian papa went out with Queen Victoria! I'm going on a holiday, that's all.'

Luka inspected her face and said quietly, 'I like Hunt and respect him, but if he hurts you I'll make him sorry he ever saw you.'

Cia rolled her eyes. 'If I'm stupid enough to let him hurt me, *I'll* deal with it, dearest cousin! I'm a woman, not a child who has to be protected.'

Luka didn't look convinced, but commanded abruptly, 'Keep in touch. Regularly!'

'I won't fall off the edge of the world.' The only way she could get through this was pretend it was another royal engagement, one that had to be endured however boring it might be. She smiled at him. 'I'm taking my laptop, so we can email each other.'

His gaze rested on Alexa's bright head, kindling. 'I own a beach house on an island just north of Auckland. I'll give you the address and the caretaker's telephone number.'

Alexa looked up, her mouth trembling into a smile. As though they'd shouted it, Cia knew that they'd consummated their love in that house—and that she'd never go there. 'Fine,' she said briskly. 'Thank you.'

Now, Luka's kisses on her cheeks and his embrace still enveloping her in familiar warmth, she walked beside Hunt into the jet without a backward glance.

He looked at her with cool speculation. 'All right?'

All right didn't describe her emotions; that would need a grand opera. Over the past week her whole life had been thrown into chaos, and she didn't even know what she felt any more. She had made a decision and she just had to keep going.

'I'm fine,' she managed to say. 'I hate saying goodbye.'

Once in the luxuriously appointed plane, she settled back into the seat and closed her burning eyes. She didn't look back as Dacia fell behind them, a brightly coloured jewel

# Get FREE BOOKS and a FREE GIFT when you play the...

# LAS VEGAS

## GAME

*Just scratch off
the gold box with a coin.
Then check below to see
the gifts you get!*

**YES!** I have scratched off the gold box. Please send me my **2 FREE BOOKS** and **gift for which I qualify.** I understand that I am under no obligation to purchase any books as explained on the back of this card.

▼ DETACH AND MAIL CARD TODAY! ▼

---

### 306 HDL DZ9V          106 HDL D2AC

FIRST NAME

LAST NAME

ADDRESS

APT.#          CITY

STATE/PROV.          ZIP/POSTAL CODE          (H-P-07/04)

| | | | |
|---|---|---|---|
| **7** | **7** | **7** | Worth TWO FREE BOOKS plus a BONUS Mystery Gift! |
| 🍒 | 🍒 | 🍒 | Worth TWO FREE BOOKS! |
| 🔔 | 🔔 | ♣ | TRY AGAIN! |

www.eHarlequin.com

in the blue, blue Mediterranean. Before long, her lashes fluttered down and she let herself drift into unconsciousness.

The long trip to New Zealand passed in a haze. As though the past months had drained every reserve of strength, Cia slept for much of the time and when she wasn't dozing or reading, she was content to watch the world slip by under their wings.

Whenever she looked for Hunt, he was working. However, he seemed to know each time she woke; he came to sit beside her and talk about nothings until she went back to sleep again. He also insisted she eat regular meals and drink plenty of water.

On the last hop she woke to find herself splayed across his chest, his arm holding her in place, his heart beating against her cheek, his subtle, sexy scent clouding her brain. For a second she froze, and wondered how on earth she could love one man and yet feel so—so safe, so secure, in the arms of another.

Nervously, she muttered, 'Sorry—I don't know—'

His broad shoulders lifted in a slight shrug. 'You were crying,' he told her. 'Bad dream?'

Her gaze collided with his, then slid sideways to the window. Biting her lip, she shook her head. 'I don't remember.'

'You looked very pathetic,' he said, a note of mockery in the deep voice. 'And I'm a sucker for tears.'

And then the simple comfort of his embrace altered in some subliminal way. Like hers, his body was reacting to hidden, involuntary signals. Desire cramped deep in the pit of her stomach, and her skin heated while the hidden places of her body prepared for him in unseen ways.

Jerking herself away, she said huskily, 'We need to talk.'

Hunt's thick lashes drooped further, unsettling what remained of her wits. 'Go ahead.' His voice was smooth.

Words tangled on her tongue. She took a deep breath and blurted, 'I don't know what you want.'

When his brows rose, she dragged in more oxygen and grabbed for the composure she'd believed had been bred in her genes. Unfortunately, now she needed it more than ever before, she could only manage a tenuous link with her usual self-assurance.

She went on baldly, 'Everything's happened so quickly. I don't—I'm not sure I want to continue the sort of relationship you might think I do.'

Oh, God, why not babble gibberish and be done with it? She started again, 'I mean—'

'I know what you mean,' he said, mercifully cutting her off before she could embarrass herself even more. 'Relax, I'm not into rape.'

'I didn't mean *that*!'

When she stared at him, great amber eyes filled with a mixture of doubt and confusion and wariness, he said less caustically, 'Don't worry, Lucia. Any decision will be yours to make.'

'Sorry,' she muttered again. 'My brain seems to have turned to custard.'

He showed his teeth in a hard smile and got to his feet. 'Perhaps you should wash your face. We're about an hour away from arrival in Auckland.'

In the bathroom Cia made running repairs, concentrating hard on reapplying cosmetics so that when she emerged into the main cabin she could meet Hunt's eyes with the confidence of having her armour fastened firmly into place.

From then on she kept a close watch through the window; as New Zealand finally began to unroll beneath the plane, she leaned forward to marvel at the vivid colour of the countryside.

A tightening of her skin warned that Hunt was taking his

place beside her. She turned. 'I'd forgotten how green a country could be.'

She flushed at his amused look and drew in a deep breath.

She needed time to herself, to find out which she really was—the woman who had loved Luka so chastely all these years, or the woman who had made passionate, ecstatic love with a man she'd known very little time at all.

The long hours of the flight had been a kind of watershed between the past and the future, but they'd convinced her that she couldn't trust herself. Erotic dreams of Hunt had plagued her sleep, and whenever he came near her body had quivered in feverish anticipation, every cell acutely poised on the edge of arousal. Waking in his arms had clinched her decision.

Staying with him would be hell. The more she gave in to this—this obsessive attraction, the less she understood herself.

Better to set her teeth and brave Luka's beach house— which didn't seem so desperately forbidding now. Distance, she thought forlornly, was working its wonders. Or perhaps she'd been fooling herself all these years, and now, literally on the other side of the world, she could see things more clearly.

In spite of the tact she'd always been rather proud of, she didn't know how to tell Hunt of her decision. In the end she said bluntly, 'I don't think it would be a good idea to stay with you.'

Black brows lifting, he looked at her. 'No?' he said after a moment that drummed with tension. 'Why not?'

*Because I want you so much my mouth dries whenever I see you, and every time you come into the room it feels as though you've sucked all the oxygen out of the air.*

Of course she didn't say it; he'd think she was mad. And he might take advantage of her admission. In his world, sex was common currency; it meant little beyond satisfying a hunger.

Cia could read nothing but dispassionate interest in his angular, forceful face, and hesitated a moment before saying sturdily, 'I just don't think it would be a good idea. I'll stay at Luka's beach house.'

'When did you work this out?'

She flushed, but met his eyes, cold and blue as a polar sky. 'Somewhere between Dacia and here.'

'No.' The word was said without expression, yet its impact made her flinch.

'I'm afraid you don't have the right to forbid it,' she pointed out with a smile she suspected ended up more placating than determined.

Hunt in a temper was intimidating.

He leaned back into the seat and said calmly, 'I promised your cousin I'd take care of you while you were in New Zealand. I have no intention of letting you swan off on your own. If you go off to the beach house I'll feel obliged to let Luka know, and I imagine he'll wonder why.'

Cia sat up very straight and said between her teeth, 'Why should you? He offered me the beach house when I told him I was coming here, so it will be all right—'

'It is not all right.' He frowned, a muscle jerking in his jaw. 'You have no idea how life functions outside the protected little enclave you've inhabited all your life.'

She flushed. 'Oh, for heaven's sake, what on earth could happen to me? I've always heard that New Zealand was safe.'

'It's safer than most countries, but I'm not thinking about home invasions or robberies.'

'Then what?'

'Paparazzi. They're already here *en masse* for Pagan

Russell's latest film, which is being shot about half an hour by water away from Luka's beach house.'

Cia recognised the name of a Hollywood star whose name had been linked with Hunt's the previous year. Pagan Russell was a glorious redhead with porcelain skin and eyes that exuded sensuous knowledge. She was also a brilliant actress.

I am not jealous, Cia thought sternly. Jealousy is an ignoble emotion and I won't give in to it.

Hunt pointed out with infuriating logic, 'The Ice Princess would be a titillating contrast to the Queen of Sex. I'd give you—oh, two hours—before the bay is filled with photographers.'

'But no one will know I'm there,' she retorted robustly.

He shrugged. 'I know what this is, of course.'

'What?' Cia asked, anger frosting her tone.

'You're afraid,' he said coolly.

Cia lifted her brows in delicate scorn. 'Afraid of what?'

He sent her a slanted look. 'Of yourself, I suspect,' he said. 'Life in a golden tower has kept you nicely insulated from all the temptations that assail the rest of us. But when I touch you—'

Cia jumped as a lean forefinger came to rest on the middle of her bottom lip. Sharp points of desire arrowed through her, drowning out everything but the remorseless goad of passion. When her eyelids sank down she had to force them up so she could glare at him.

Only to fall headlong into icy hunger, into a darkness that threatened everything she was…

'Don't,' she said hoarsely, her mouth so parched she could barely get the word out.

'When I touch you,' he said with ruthless honesty, 'or come near you, or even walk into the same room, you realise that you're not able to control me. Or yourself.' He smiled and removed that taunting finger to lean back into his seat, all aloof, maddening authority. 'And as you're a control freak, it scares you.'

'Lust happens,' she returned, trying hard to sound frivolous.

Hunt's narrowed eyes—crystalline jewels in his lean, dark face—glinted with cold scorn. 'It's a normal reaction between normal people,' he said, turning his head so that all she saw was his profile, hawk-angled against the bright sun of New Zealand. 'But you'll be quite safe at Hinekura. I'll give you a key so you don't have to spend nights waiting for my footsteps at your door.'

She said stiffly, 'I'm not afraid of that. Or of you.' He wanted her, but he wasn't like her, tangled in a net of passion. He could control it.

'And you'll be quite safe from yourself,' he promised, his voice lazily amused. 'As safe as you want to be.'

'That is such a big deal,' she said venomously.

He laughed. 'Relax. You're a grown woman, not a blushing virgin.'

No longer. Stung, and hugely embarrassed, Cia leaned back in her seat and watched with blind absorption the vibrant green countryside of New Zealand slip silently beneath.

Of course he couldn't force her to go with him. If he tried she'd simply go to the nearest security person at the airport and ask for protection. Plutocrats shared with royalty a hatred of the wrong sort of publicity. Once Hunt realised that she wasn't going with him, he'd give up.

He'd have to.

But another glance at that strong profile ate into her confidence.

After clearing Immigration and Customs they were met by a young man with red hair and a respectful smile.

'Airport security suggests you leave by a private exit, Mr Radcliffe,' he said, indicating a door. 'There are photographers lying in wait.'

Without breaking stride Hunt took Cia's elbow and steered her through the door and down a corridor. 'For us?' he asked.

His aide said smoothly, 'They know the princess is accompanying you, sir. I've taken the precaution of having a limo lurk inconspicuously around the corner as a decoy, and the chopper's geared up and ready to go.'

When he turned to speak to the security man, Cia said something under her breath.

'Exactly.' Hunt's voice was crisp and unemotional.

She risked a swift upward glance. 'You don't speak Dacian.'

'I understand swearing when I hear it in any language,' he said with a slashing white grin.

Unwillingly she smiled back. 'I gather this isn't your usual welcome when you come home?'

'No.'

Cia frowned. 'I wonder how they found out I was coming to New Zealand with you.'

'There are probably tabloid stringers on Dacia. It wouldn't have been difficult to find out that you were leaving with me.'

'No one on Dacia would do that,' she said indignantly.

Hunt's beautiful mouth compressed into an uncompromising line. 'Welcome to the real world, princess. Tabloids pay good money for information. There's a huge, high-paying market for pictures of royalty—especially young, beautiful princesses on holiday with men who are neither brothers nor fiancés. Your cousin controls the situation in Dacia, but once you stepped off the island you moved out of his sphere of influence.'

She retorted tartly, 'And your highly publicised affair with Pagan Russell last year would have set them quivering with anticipation. Where are we going?'

Hunt shrugged. 'We're taking the helicopter to another airport where we'll go straight to my plane. Once we're at Hinekura no one will bother us.'

'Why not?' Only when the words had left her lips did Cia realise she'd tacitly accepted his right to hijack her.

'We don't cater to prying photographers in the far north.'

The note of cold determination in his voice sent a shiver across the sensitive spot between her shoulder blades. Staring straight ahead, she said, 'How do you manage that?'

'The road is fifteen kilometres away through my land. And I don't like trespassers.'

She said, 'How long is Pagan Russell going to be here?'

'I have no idea.'

Chilled, she ploughed on, 'I'll go to the beach house once things settle down.'

Hunt released her elbow as they came through the door into the sunlight. 'OK, here's the helicopter. Get in.'

While Cia scrambled into the back seat he and the aide and the security man heaved their luggage into the boot, then Hunt slid in beside her and the chopper immediately pulled away.

# CHAPTER SEVEN

SETTLING back into the helicopter seat—too small to be comfortable, as they all were—Hunt regarded Lucia's classical profile, his loins stirring at the silken glory of her skin and the elegant curves of that sultry mouth. Was she as naïve as she seemed to be?

Probably. Her cousin's protectiveness and the Dacians' affection had sheltered her from the worst excesses of the gutter Press; here she'd be a spicy sitting duck.

He assessed the slight tinge of pink along those stunning cheekbones. She knew he was watching her. The lush mouth compressed and she turned her head away so that all he could see was the curve of her cheek and her ear. A small diamond stud winked in the lobe.

A swift surge of passion infuriated him. How the hell had he managed to get himself into this situation? If he'd had any sense he'd let her go to Luka's beach house. Hell, if he'd had any sense he wouldn't have slept with her in the first place, and he certainly wouldn't have allowed himself to invite her back home.

He'd always been careful not to involve himself in messy situations with the women in his life, yet his stupid, reckless impulse, prompted by her reaction to Alexa's bombshell, had led to her presence in his house for at least a week.

He noted the black hair primly smoothed back from her serene features. The night they'd made love he'd pulled it from its knot, and let it tumble in a silken flood across his chest...

Ruthlessly he yanked his mind above his belt. Apart from

that, he knew very little about Lucia Bagaton. She was intelligent; she had all the qualities she needed for the position she'd inherited.

And one second of shock had told him how she felt about being relegated to the background. Apart from that, her regal air of composure was seamless—except in his arms.

Since the age of sixteen he'd had no problems attracting the opposite sex. In fact, while he was still at high school a woman of thirty had taught him how to play the stock market. That wasn't all she'd taught him, but it had laid the foundation for his future. He'd learned how women thought, and how they felt. Was that why he was so attracted to a woman who gave nothing away?

Think of it as a new experience, he advised himself cynically.

He glanced down as the chopper started to lose height. He knew one other thing about her; in spite of her antagonism, she wanted him every bit as he wanted her. And he'd never asked any more of a woman than that.

So why the desire to throttle her?

No paparazzi lay in wait for them at the much smaller airport. As they walked from the chopper towards the private plane that waited for them, Lucia asked suddenly, 'What does the name of your farm—station—mean? Hinekura?'

'Excellent pronunciation,' he drawled.

She shrugged. 'The vowel sounds are the same as Italian.'

'It's made up of two words—*hine*, meaning woman or girl, and *kura*, meaning beautiful. In other words, beautiful woman.'

'Is there a story?'

He repeated the words she'd used to him when they'd gone to the cave, the first time he'd kissed her. 'There's always a story. It was once the home of a woman of such exquisite beauty that she caused a vast amount of trouble. Neighbouring chiefs fought over her, and even when she married, men tried to abduct her. In the end she caused such turmoil that her husband, clearly a pragmatist, killed her.'

Cia's stomach contracted. 'A much grimmer story than the one I told you,' she said politely, then added, 'Hunt, I don't want you to think that I'm ungrateful when I say I'd rather go to the beach house.'

She wondered why he was scrutinising her face, his long lashes hiding everything of his eyes but a narrow, lethal line of steel.

But when he spoke his voice was negligent. 'It's not a good option. You're too exposed at the beach.'

Stupid colour stung her cheeks. 'Exposed?'

'Too easy to get at. Paparazzi are noted for their ingenuity, and New Zealand's small enough for someone to let slip that you're in residence. They could land from the sea, and in New Zealand it's perfectly legal to walk below the high-tide mark. I doubt if you'd enjoy having them camped out on the beach with telephoto lenses.'

Frustrated and uneasy, she bit her lip. 'Of course I wouldn't. But I won't impose on you for very long.'

They stopped beside the plane. In ten minutes Cia was staring out of the window at Auckland's twin harbours. Hunt sat in the front, talking to the pilot as the plane flew high above the long northern peninsula, and eventually her lashes fluttered down and she drifted off into a kind of half-waking, half-sleeping trance.

An alteration to the engine noise stirred her, as did the bump of their landing, but she found it almost impossible to lift her lashes. A kind of fearful excitement possessed her; she felt that when she opened her eyes and saw Hunt's home everything would change, as though she'd crossed some forbidden border into dangerous, unknown territory. Once she'd arrived, she'd be unable to go back.

'Lucia, we're here,' Hunt said quietly into the sudden silence when the engines were cut.

Eyes still shut, she yawned and nodded.

He laughed. 'I'll carry you.'

The same words Luka had used—how long ago? She couldn't recall. Delivered without Luka's love for Alexa and in Hunt's deep, cool voice, they chilled her.

Cia forced up her eyelids to say with dignity, 'I'm not usually such a sleepyhead; I can walk, thank you.'

To prove it she unclipped her seat belt and got up, only to stagger slightly. Hunt's arms came around her in support, and she looked up into hooded eyes, glittering in his tanned face.

Her bones melted, and in the silence of the plane she heard her heart thud rapidly in her ears.

Then she was free. Her lips felt stiff as she said, 'Thank you.'

He stood back. 'My pleasure.' The deep voice was level and completely without emotion.

As warily as a cat, Cia climbed down the steps onto the airstrip, a mown stretch of grass running gently up to the crest of a hill; waiting a short distance away was a four-wheel-drive vehicle spattered with red mud. As she watched, it backed up to the plane.

The driver was a woman a few years older than Cia. She greeted Hunt with every appearance of pleasure and sent a swift smile Cia's way before seizing a small package from the pilot and loading it into the back of the vehicle.

Too late, Cia realised that she should have offered to help, but between the pilot, Hunt and the woman, it was clearly a well-rehearsed procedure; the woman dealt with the smaller parcels while men carried the heavy stuff.

Oppressed by a chill of alienation, Cia looked past the half-round hangar made of corrugated iron. The hill sloped gently towards the east before falling away sharply to a coastal plain, now gathering a blue-grey cloak as twilight swept across it. Sunlight still gleamed on the sea, turning it to a slab of polished silver under a cloudy sky. Green, lushly beautiful, Hinekura was as different from Dacia as any place could be. A great, shivering wave of homesickness rolled over her.

'Hop into the Range Rover,' Hunt said. When she stared at him he picked her up and dumped her into the back seat.

Feeling like a recalcitrant child, she sat up very straight and watched as he and the woman got into the front, Hunt behind the wheel. He turned slightly and said, 'Lucia, this is Sheree Anderson, who runs my office for me.'

After a quick exchange of greetings he switched on the engine, frowning as the woman began to talk.

Cia heard a few words—'can't be helped,' and 'I'm so sorry, Hunt, but there's nothing else I can do,' and 'tomorrow.'

She looked away as Hunt spoke swiftly and decisively. The road wound down a steep hillside, a narrow red-brown gash between dense, heavily leafed trees that looked like jungle. Great Catherine wheels of delicate fern fronds sprang from rough black trunks, and in the dimness beneath the trees more growth pushed towards the light, eager and fecund and riotous.

The woman in front nodded, and the vehicle burst out onto a wide rolling area covered in bright grass. Huge, stolid red cattle lifted their heads to watch the vehicle go past. In the distance Cia caught glimpses of houses sheltered by trees, and other buildings.

Another wave of homesickness drenched her. It looked

wild and different and exotic—in truth, a world away from all she knew and loved.

She sat up straight. OK, so she'd clutched at Hunt's offer of sanctuary without thinking past her need to convince Luka—and Alexa—that she wasn't pining. Coming here had been risky, but she trusted Hunt to keep his promise.

Making love to him had been crazy; she didn't regret it, but repeating it would be rushing rashly into a situation she couldn't control. Ignoring the swift thud of her pulses in her ears, she forced herself to gaze around at the empty land and the strong lines of the hills, so utterly different from Dacia and England, so alien…

Hunt drew up outside a high hedge of trees cut by a long metal gate; without killing the engine, he said, 'All right, see what you can do, Sheree, and let me know as soon as you can. If you need any help, tell me.'

'I should be able to give you a straight answer tonight,' the woman said, flashed a smile at Cia, and left them, running through the gate between big, fat drops of rain from a dark cloud overhead.

Hunt glanced in the rear-vision mirror. 'All right?'

Something sharp and barbed pierced Cia's heart. 'Fine, thank you,' she said prosaically.

He put the vehicle in gear and drove along the narrow road towards a collection of buildings. As the rain stopped he turned off onto a long drive beneath a tunnel of trees.

When they left the shelter of the avenue the house swung into view. Eyes widening, Cia stared and leaned forward.

'It's beautiful,' she breathed. 'Like a miracle.'

Hunt had excellent hearing. 'What's miraculous about it?'

'Finding a house like this here in the wilderness.'

'New Zealand does a much better wilderness than this,' he said coolly.

Cia sat back and admired the gardens as the Range Rover

climbed a low rise between lawns gleaming silver with rain. And such a house! Mediterranean in style, but she glimpsed huge walls of glass, and was sure she saw a long deck or terrace. Cia drew in a sharp breath and looked down as the noise of the wheels changed.

They were crossing a bridge over a narrow, rock-bound stream; judging by its direction, the stream passed very close to the house. Trees followed its banks, and exotic plants sheltered between the huge rocks. She saw familiar ones— the long, scented trumpets of datura, and the sensuous splash of hibiscuses.

The drive led past a big front door, but the Range Rover swept onto a gravel courtyard behind the house bordered by a high wall and a large garage.

'Home,' Hunt said laconically as he killed the engine. 'I'll take you straight in—you're whacked.'

It was true. 'Why aren't you?' she asked crossly, undoing her seat belt and clambering out.

'I'm used to air travel, but even so, jet lag is insidious. I didn't pilot the plane up because I don't trust myself after a long flight.' He looked at her. 'Can you walk?'

'Of course I can,' she said with dignity, demonstrating by taking a few steps away from the vehicle.

Hunt escorted her along a covered walkway and through a door in the wall into a large courtyard. A flash of green proclaimed a swimming pool; Cia noted roses and dahlias and the vivid blossoms of bougainvillea, the familiar flowers and scents easing some of her loneliness.

They were met halfway by a large, stately woman with keen dark eyes and a pleasant smile.

He introduced her as Marty, the housekeeper. She smiled at Cia and said, 'Welcome to Hinekura.' The name ran off her tongue like liquid silver, smooth and rhythmic. 'I hope you had a good journey.'

'Thank you, I did.' But by now tension was clutching her in a grip of iron.

Inside the house, she relaxed a little. Airy and modern, it achieved both warmth and grace. And it fitted its formidable owner; yes, she thought, taking in a superb abstract picture on one wall, this belongs here, with Hunt.

It looked as different from Dacia as anything could be.

'What a lovely house,' she said brightly and inanely, all her glib small talk left behind in Dacia.

From behind Hunt said, 'I'll tell the architect and designer you liked it.'

He sounded fed up. She bit her lip but persevered, 'How long have you lived here?'

'Six years.' He turned to the housekeeper. 'I'll take Lucia up to her room.'

At the top of the stairs he opened a door. 'In here.'

Cia walked in and after a quick glance around said even more brightly, 'Thank you.'

'Your bags will be up shortly. Marty will unpack for you—'

'Oh, there's no need for that,' she said, smiling dangerously. 'I know how to unlock my bags and I can see a door over there that must lead to a wardrobe. Possibly even a bathroom? Hanging things up won't tax my strength too much, I'm sure.'

Blue fire glinted in his eyes above a smile that mocked her combativeness. 'I'd suggest a shower and a nap if you feel like it. Dinner is at seven, but for the next couple of hours I'm going to be busy in the office. If you're hungry, Marty will get you something to drink and eat.'

'I don't—'

'I'd suggest that you at least drink some water to rehydrate. If you'd like to, I can take you out to see the horses before dinner,' he finished smoothly.

Her hand sought reassurance from the diamond star, but dropped when she remembered it was now hidden in her luggage, never to be worn again. Meeting his hard eyes with a lift of her chin, she said, 'You've got horses here? I thought all farms in New Zealand were completely mechanised.'

'You have done your homework,' he said admiringly. 'This is a hill station. We use quad bikes where we can, but a lot of the land is too rugged for them, so horses are necessary. I'll see you later.'

She waited until the door closed behind him before exhaling forcefully. For a few seconds there she'd felt a chilling draught, like a blast from the north pole. In this hemisphere it would be the south pole, she corrected herself, and went across the room to the door on the far side. It led to a big, airy wardrobe with a bathroom next door.

A bathroom made for luxury. Cia examined the smooth, flowing lines of the fixtures, the soft rose and cream marble, thick towels, deliciously scented soaps, a vase of flowers picked from the garden.

Entirely suitable for a self-made millionaire, she told herself, angry at the snide comment the minute it had formed in her brain. Hunt had taken what he was born with and transformed his life; she doubted very much whether he cared much about his surroundings, although she liked the restrained luxury she'd seen so far.

Sudden tears blinded her. She wiped her eyes and blew her nose, and told herself that she was embarking on a new stage of her life. Surely once the turmoil inside her had settled she'd be whole again.

In the meantime, she wanted nothing more than a long, hot shower and a complete change of clothes.

A knock on the outer door heralded the arrival of her

cases. 'You must be Peter,' she said as she let in the man who carried them. 'Thanks so much.'

He was stocky and middle-aged, his muscles rippling when he put the cases on the floor at the foot of the huge bed.

'I'm Peter,' he agreed cheerfully. 'Marty said to tell you that if you need anything, just call on the phone and she'll be up straight away.'

'I'm sure she's too busy to be climbing the stairs,' Cia said. 'I can come down if I need anything.'

He grinned. 'There's a lift,' he confided. 'Don't worry about Marty—she'll tell you if she's too busy.'

When Cia laughed his grin widened. 'See you later,' he said cheerfully, and left her.

A couple of hours later Cia had unpacked, ironed the creases from her clothes, and indulged in a long, long shower. Although Luka had modernised the island's water supplies, living on Dacia meant embracing the saving of water as an art form. Here there might be greater leeway. She glanced out of the window as more rain, heavier this time, shadowed the garden and dashed drops against the windows.

'We don't encourage anyone to waste water, but we don't have a shortage. We have bores,' Hunt told her later that night in the dining room.

Cia laughed. 'So does every place, alas. What do bores have to do with the water supply?'

'We bore down into an underground spring or stream and pump the water into tanks for filtering. Also, we collect rainwater from the roofs of the buildings.' Wind pounced on the house again, hurling a stinging fusillade across the windows. Hunt added drily, 'As you may have noticed, it rains a lot here.'

'It's very different from Dacia,' she said, swirling the last of a glass of water in the bottom of her goblet. For some reason she hadn't wanted wine tonight, but Hunt had drunk a glass of red with his meal. 'Our rain comes in winter, with very little for the rest of the year.'

'We do have droughts, but not often, not in the north.' His tone was aloof and she glanced up.

The candles in the centre of the table guttered a little, and the flickering light played over his face, highlighting the magnificent bone structure that would make him a striking man all his life. She remembered how he had looked the night they made love, and sensation collected in a pool of sensuous heat at the base of her spine.

All evening she'd been fighting a rising tide of excitement. This was the first time she'd eaten a meal alone with him—almost the first time they'd been alone together except for that night.

She'd tried to push the memory away, but it came back to torment her, vagrant images suddenly blazing like beacons, dissolving her brain into a loose collection of desires driven by compelling hunger.

'Such a temperate climate must make farming as easy as it gets,' she said, aware of a slight roughening in her voice.

'In many ways. We fight diseases, of course, and idiots who try to bring in food and other stuffs made from animals without declaring them. New Zealand is finding that although it is so far from the rest of the world it can't hold everything bad in it at bay.' He looked directly at her and said softly, 'But that's not a particularly interesting subject.'

'I find it very interesting,' she said indignantly. 'Luka—'

She stopped, because his raised brows and half-closed eyes sent a chill through her.

'Luka?' he said politely, and finished the rest of his wine in one swallow, setting the glass down with a slight clink against his dinner plate.

'Luka discussed such things with me,' she said with cool detachment, wishing she could retire behind the temporary, cowardly shield of a wine glass. Instead, she lifted her chin and met his gaze steadily.

'And now,' he said blandly, 'he discusses them with Alexa.'

'Yes.'

Humiliation gripped her, hollowing out her stomach until all she could feel was cold shame. However, it was none of Hunt's business who she loved. Unlike poor Maxime, he hadn't asked for anything more than a night of passion.

And he'd got that, she thought, all the fire suddenly quenched.

If his ego needed stroking, her response surely had been enough.

She bit her lip as it occurred to her that part of the reason for her turmoil was exactly that—he'd wanted nothing more from her than the temporary loan of her body and its responses. She hated herself for her hypocrisy; she was in love with Luka, yet she wanted Hunt to feel more for her than lust.

He said, 'I'm sorry we missed out on visiting the horses this afternoon. My secretary has had health problems, so I had to do some catching up. And although I'm reasonably fast on the computer, I'm not as good as she is.'

Impetuously Cia said, 'Can I do something? I'm excellent on a computer.'

He regarded her with a twisted smile. 'Are you?' he said. 'This is a little different from keeping a social diary and writing the occasional letter for your cousin to sign.'

Cia bristled. 'Oh, I can do a little more than that,' she said sweetly.

The minute she'd said she might be able to help she'd regretted such rashness—after all, she'd planned to head off to Luka's beach house as soon as it was safe. However, in the face of that patronising comment she'd show him.

'We can give it a try to see how it goes,' he said slowly.

'Certainly. You must tell me if I'm hopeless,' she returned, and only then wondered if she'd been manipulated into this offer.

A glance at Hunt dampened that idea. He planned to give her a chance to show how far out of her depth she was, and then no doubt he'd summon one of a hoard of secretaries or personal assistants or aides he had at his fingertips.

'Done,' he said, and held out a hand.

Cia extended her own, shocked when he lifted it to his mouth. Warm, persuasive, his lips touched the soft skin on the back of her hand in a formal European salute, then, setting her heart pounding madly, he turned it over and kissed the palm, folding her fingers over the spot.

'Thank you,' he said as she retrieved it. He looked up and said, 'Ah, here comes Marty.'

Intensely grateful for the housekeeper's entrance, Cia folded her hands in her lap, but those kisses burned in her mind long after she'd sampled the splendid cheeses and fruit that finished the meal.

And that night Hunt invaded her dreams again until she woke, panting with erotic need, her whole body screaming with frustration when she opened her eyes into the cold, lonely darkness.

Eventually she went back to sleep, but was pulled out of her dreams by sunlight on the curtains and the enthusiastic song of birds. She lay listening to one that sounded like a peal of bells, then got out and padded across to the window, pushing back the curtains to peer out.

She didn't catch sight of the bird that sounded like a carillon, but across a splendid sweep of lawn and a dense border of trees, where raindrops refracted the sun's light into diamond points, she saw a man on a horse.

Hunt. How on earth did he learn to ride like that? Her breath came shortly through her lips and she leaned out into air so clear and fresh it was like diving into the sea on a hot day. He was riding a horse the same rich mahogany as his hair, either a stallion or a gelding.

Cia had been around horses since she was a child, but except in competitions she'd rarely seen anyone so powerfully attuned to his mount. Together they looked like a centaur, the mythic man-horse of ancient Mediterranean legend.

'Perhaps it's in the genes?' she asked him over breakfast.

He shrugged. 'I doubt it, although I learned to ride before I could walk. As you probably know, my father was a trainer, so I grew up around horses and stables.'

'Life must have been difficult with both parents gone.'

'I never knew my mother.'

'I'm sorry,' she said inadequately. Introduced to drugs by a lover after her marriage broke up, her own mother had been pretty useless, but Cia had always known that she loved her.

His glance was keen. 'Apparently she had an affair with my father then disappeared, only to reappear nine months later with me. My father didn't know whether or not I was his child, but he accepted responsibility. I think he loved her.'

'I'd have liked to meet your father,' Cia said calmly, above a seething outrage that anyone could do that to a child they'd borne. 'He sounds a gallant gentleman.'

He gave a cool smile. 'You'd have had nothing in common. He was tough and foul-mouthed and he was a gambler—although always within limits. He loved horses and me in that order, but he did his best for me.'

'I'll bet he was proud of the son he raised,' she said firmly, pouring very rich milk into her tea.

'He'd have certainly approved of the way I got my start,' he said sardonically.

She laughed. 'Trading in penny dreadfuls? You really have to know what you're doing.'

Hunt's brows shot up. 'You did some in-depth research,' he said softly.

Her smile congealed. 'Research is a necessary part of modern business.'

'Modern business, yes, but we have no business together. Did you want to find out if I knew which fork to use?'

Coolly, denying his right to demand an answer, she said, 'I did a lot of Luka's research. And no, the question of forks never came up.'

An odd little silence—tense with unspoken emotions—prickled between them. He broke it. 'I'm not ashamed of getting my start that way, but moving in and out of the sharemarket day by day, buying cheap shares low and selling them a little higher, comes very close to gambling.'

Cia nodded. 'But like your father you knew when to stop.'

He drank some coffee, watching her as he did so. When he'd set down the cup he said, 'Like you, I did a lot of research. What else did you learn about me?'

Well, the names of his mistresses and the duration of each one's stay in his bed, for one. She said evenly, 'Don't worry, I only used reputable sources.'

The smile curving his mouth came close to a taunt. 'Ever diplomatic. I dislike appearing in the Press so I take care not to give them too much fodder for speculation.' He glanced at his watch and got to his feet, towering over the table in instant, automatic domination. 'I'll see you in the office in an hour.'

# CHAPTER EIGHT

'AN HOUR? Of course.' Cia got up from the table and walked across to a wall of glass that opened onto a wide terrace. 'Whose idea was it to build on the edge of the stream?'

Hunt rose to accompany her out into the warm sunlight. 'Mine.'

Cia wasn't surprised. The architect who'd designed the house had been brilliant, but the house showed signs of constant input from the client. Every picture she saw, every colour and pattern and arrangement of furniture reinforced Hunt's personality, brushing against her nerves like an invisible velvet cloak—tactile, potent, seductive.

She walked across to the railing and looked down. Immediately below, the little rushing brook found its way between smooth, rounded boulders, its music a jingling counterpoint to the song of birds.

She sighed. 'It smells so fresh here—like a new day. I love the way the house is surrounded by forest, and yet the sun pours in. And those tree-ferns are truly spectacular.'

He was watching her; even with her back to him she could feel his attention. In fact, she thought, looking into the green depths of the trees, she felt new-born herself, as though she'd shed a skin and been transformed. Her tiredness had dropped away, leaving her senses singing.

From behind Hunt said, 'Later you might like to swim. The pool is kept at a constant temperature.'

'That would be lovely,' she returned politely, and smiled over her shoulder.

Blue-sheened eyes held hers. Often enough, Cia had heard people say that the world stood still; she took it for a tired old cliché, but now she knew what it meant. Everything froze; she heard nothing but the beating of her own heart, felt nothing but the impact of Hunt's gaze, and saw nothing but the hard, striking face with its fierce cheekbones and the mouth that took her to ecstasy.

'Lucia, stop it,' he said harshly.

The world began to move again; birds sang above the sound of water, a slight breeze caressed her bare arms, her insides reassembled themselves into a functioning body. She shook her head numbly, tensing as he came up to her.

'I don't know whether you're a tease or just incredibly naïve,' he said beneath his breath, and bent his head and kissed her as though driven by an imperative desire beyond his control.

After a shocked moment, Cia's mouth softened under his. This was what she'd been waiting for since the night they'd made love, she realised dazedly. Her arms stole up around his neck and she responded with a desire that matched his, lost to everything but the taste of him and the texture of his body against hers, his arms around her, his hair against her fingertips.

He lifted his head and asked harshly, 'Which are you, Lucia? Temptress or innocent?'

'You know I'm not an innocent,' she whispered, skin burning at memories of the night she'd spent in his arms. Her body ached with feverish hunger and it took every bit of composure she possessed to allow her to say, 'But I don't think I'm a temptress, either. Do I have to be one or the other?'

He kissed her again—lightly, with tantalising expertise this time—and then stepped back, a humourless smile bracketing his beautiful mouth. 'You'd better go for that walk,' he said quietly, 'before I carry you up to my bedroom.'

He'd reimposed control so easily; it took Cia half an hour of exploring the magnificent grounds to put a fragile leash on her emotions. She felt as though she was on the verge of some magnificent discovery—as though life had suddenly given her a rare and precious gift, and she needed only to accept it to find herself.

'In other words,' she told herself severely as she checked out a tennis court hidden behind a tangle of profuse growth, 'you're letting yourself get carried away by a man who only has to kiss your hand to get your blood pressure steaming out of your ears! He might make love like—well, like one of the old gods, but he changes lovers every year or so.'

She stopped, and smelt a late rose, realising with stark insight how close she'd come to admitting that she wanted more from Hunt than sex.

It would be so easy to just drift along and let this over-whelming passion take her where it wanted, she thought longingly. But it would be dangerously reckless.

She had a life to make, things to do, a career to plan, and it wasn't Hunt's fault that these seemed suddenly hollow ambitions. Because she'd first experienced sex with him, she'd always remember him as the man who had shown her a whole new other side of herself.

But it had been nothing more than a temporary aberration.

A pale smile tugged at her lips. *Aberration?* Now that was a stiff word for mind-blowing eroticism!

It was the truth, though, and she had to face it. In his arms she'd tasted heaven, but he'd said nothing about any future for them.

And she was beginning to want one. If she stayed around too long, she might commit another unforgivably stupid act and become addicted to him.

Firming her mouth, she glanced at her watch and turned back to the house.

Hunt's office was exactly that—a large room holding everything the modern tycoon needed to run a world-spanning empire. Although Luka had insisted on the most modern equipment, and using Guy's software had given her the knowledge to hold up her end in conversations about information technology, Cia was impressed.

When she commented on it, Hunt said casually, 'I choose to live in New Zealand, so I make sure I have everything I—and my employees—need to keep in the closest contact. I've left letters for you to type on the dictaphone.'

Very cool, very businesslike.

So? she thought, seating herself at an ergonomically-designed desk and a chair that looked as though the user needed a pilot's licence to run it. You offered to do this, and you'd hate it if he treated you like a piece of fluff.

She began to type, glad now that after leaving school she'd insisted on doing a secretarial course at a high-powered technical academy.

For ten minutes or so Hunt kept a close watch on her, only relaxing when he saw that she knew how to use a computer. However, he couldn't concentrate on the papers that needed his attention. Every movement she made, every sound from her, sent signals to his libido.

So now you know why you've never had a lover share your office before, he thought irritably. Forget about long, sleek legs and that passionate mouth—and forget that she's also sharing your house, and would share your bed if you wooed her.

What did she want—the man or the position? It had never mattered before. He'd never brought a lover here before, either. Now he realised that he'd wanted to find out how she dealt with surroundings so different from the ones she was used to.

In other words, he thought, dragging his eyes back from her profile, you're testing her. Why?

Half an hour later he looked up from his desk and frowned. She hadn't adjusted the chair, and Sheree was at least four inches taller.

'You're going to get a stiff neck,' he said, getting to his feet before he could stop himself. Angry at his inability to keep his distance, he came over and bent to twist a knob.

Her faint, sensuous perfume drifted into his brain, clouding it and opening the door to a rush of memories. His body hardened. Just as well he was standing slightly behind her. 'Tell me when it feels comfortable,' he said shortly.

She answered equally abruptly. 'Just show me which levers do what and I'll get it right.'

But a note in her voice and a rush of colour along the vulnerable back of her neck told him she was as aware of him as he was of her. A rush of sheer male possessiveness drove through him, shredding his will.

Straightening up, he stepped backwards. 'That knob adjusts for your back—yes, that's it. Now for your neck—no, not there.' He reached for the knob at the same time as she did, and their hands collided.

Damn, he should have let her fix the chair by herself. Unable to resist, Hunt turned the chair so that he could scan her face. Satisfaction geared up a notch as he read in her gold, tiger-coloured eyes a hunger as devouring and mindless as his. For three heartbeats his will held, but then he said something—her name, he thought—and drew her fragrant slenderness out of the chair before he took her soft, parted lips.

He broke off the kiss when his legs threatened to give way, but he couldn't let her go. Lucia looked as dazed as he felt, as lost to the heady, mind-altering power of their desire. If he had any sense he'd send her straight off to the beach house—but for the first time ever he was a prisoner of a passion he couldn't master.

With a muffled curse, he took that soft, inviting mouth again.

Cia shuddered; the craving to touch him, feel him, taste him again had been building for too long. She opened her mouth beneath his, recklessly surrendering to the skilful, devouring exploration that stoked her passionate hunger to a dangerous inferno.

She burned where his hand slid beneath the tail of her shirt, stroking across the skin at her waist, long fingers playing delicately on the vertebrae of her spine and sending sensuous shivers its length.

Deep in the spell of his kisses, she mimicked his action, but pushed her hands up beneath his shirt to splay across his shoulders, relishing the way the powerful muscles shifted beneath the sleek, hot skin. She thought dazedly that he was all around her, all power and grace and glory...

His mouth drifted down until it found the vulnerable hollow of her throat, and his hand drifted up, but only as far as her breast, shaping it with infinite care. The small nipple budded sharply, sending a shaft of exquisite fire to the pit of her stomach. Tempted beyond endurance, she fought to retrieve a sliver of control.

Every part of her resisted the cold voice of common sense, but eventually she managed to mutter hoarsely, 'Hunt, no—'

It sounded like a plea. He lifted his head and she almost forgot whatever she'd planned to say in the glittering intensity of his gaze.

'What is it?' His voice was as guttural as hers, stripped of everything but the need to drive headlong to satisfaction.

'I don't think this is a good idea,' she said forlornly, knowing how silly it sounded, knowing that if he kissed her again she would give in and do whatever he wanted wherever he wanted—here on the desk if that was what he wanted.

Every muscle in his big body went rock-solid for a fraction of a second before he dropped his arms to his sides and stepped back. 'It seems a damned good idea to me,' he said lethally.

'Now, perhaps, but you swore just before you kissed me—and I know exactly how you feel.'

The dangerous, leaping lights in his eyes turned wry. His smile turned from feral to real, if reluctant, humour. 'Like being hit by a runaway bus,' he said. 'Only good.'

Although it was perilously sweet to share a moment of amusement with him, she struggled for the words to tell him it mustn't happen again. Finally she said, 'It scares me.'

He frowned. 'Why?'

'I'm not scared of you,' she said quickly. 'I know you wouldn't hurt me.'

But she couldn't go on and tell him that she was terrified of her own response and total lack of will-power where he was concerned. One touch, and she threw everything she'd ever learned out of the window and surrendered to this fiercely carnal longing.

He surveyed her with narrowed eyes until she could bear it no longer and turned away. Then he strode across to the window and looked out of it for long moments.

'All right,' he said curtly without facing her. 'Just keep out of my way from now on.'

'If you'll keep out of mine,' she retorted.

He shrugged. 'We'll adopt a policy of non-contact, and no, we won't shake on it.'

Relieved, yet unaccountably depressed, Cia went back to

setting the chair for her own comfort. For the rest of the morning they worked in silence, a silence that buzzed with dangerous tension.

When a clock chimed midday she glanced at her watch with surprise. A swift glance revealed Hunt leaning back in his chair, rubbing a long-fingered hand across his eyes as he stared at the screen of his own computer. An odd pang—surely not of tenderness?—shot through her, so strong she had to stop herself from getting up and bending to kiss the lines away.

'Lunch time,' he said, looking up as though her thought had been communicated to him. His mouth hardened and he got up, long body moving with the elegant economy of a predator. 'Marty gets uptight if we don't eat on time, so you'd better back up and close down now.'

More worried by that stray pang of tenderness than by her blatant physical response, Cia went through the process of backing up and shut down her computer.

When she stood up tiredness caught her unexpectedly, and she staggered.

Frowning, he ordered, 'Make sure you stand up and move around every half hour or so.'

'Yes,' she said quietly, and escaped to wash her hands.

It wasn't the work that tired her, she thought in the exquisite little powder room, it was the strain of being in the same room as Hunt. Had he felt it? It didn't seem so; she'd sneaked the occasional glance at him and felt piqued when each time he'd clearly been totally concentrating on whatever he was doing.

Whereas she, idiot that she was, registered every movement, every time he shuffled papers, every time he got to his feet to consult a file or a book, her body responding with a helpless, mindless intensity that made a mockery of her trademark composure.

Drying her hands, she thought mordantly that it was just as well he was too far away across the office for her to hear his breathing, or she'd have been obsessing about that too.

She covered a yawn and stared at her face for a second. Her restless night had painted shadows under her eyes, but she still felt that alert, vital rush of expectancy. Both shadows and weariness would disappear after another night's sleep.

After a delicious lunch Hunt said, 'Would you like to ride? It's a glorious day, and I'd like to see you on a horse.'

Perhaps some of the fresh, crisp air would clear her head. 'Love to,' she said.

'Put on a windcheater, or a jersey; there's often a wind up here. And a hat of some sort, because although you're used to putting sunscreen on in Dacia, New Zealand is directly under the hole in the ozone layer.'

Coins of colour burned along her cheekbones. He was remembering his comments just before she'd flippantly told him that sunscreen was the predominant scent in Dacia.

*Skin the colour and texture of pale gold satin, and eyes like hot amber...*

And afterwards he'd said, *As for your skin—don't tell me you don't know that every man who sees it wonders how it would look against his...*

Well, now she knew how it looked against his—gold against bronze—and the memory wrenched her heart and sent complex, tantalising shudders of sensation through her. Without looking at him she said lightly, 'Yes, of course.'

'Have you got boots?'

She nodded. 'Not riding boots, but something that will do.'

'I'll see you in half an hour.'

Brows rising, she looked at him. 'If you're giving me half

an hour to get ready,' she returned with delicate precision, 'I can be down in ten minutes.'

His brows rose. 'Fifteen.'

Suddenly light-hearted, she said, 'Done!'

They walked down to a large barn that held a tack room, and while Cia looked with interest at various items there Hunt took down two bridles and saddles. 'I'll carry something.' She held out a hand.

He hesitated and she said crisply, 'I'm not made of sugar, Hunt!'

Smiling, he handed over the bridles. 'Take those.'

Four horses and a large sheep grazed in a paddock close by; as Hunt and Cia came up the wire they all lifted their heads curiously and came ambling across.

'Feed the sheep first,' Hunt advised. 'Otherwise he's a damned nuisance.'

Cia held out her hand and let the sheep take several nuts from her palm. It removed them quickly and efficiently, its lips tickling her skin. 'What's the sheep doing in the horse paddock?'

'He used to be a pet lamb, so he doesn't think of himself as a sheep. He and Mike became best mates, and the others tolerate him.'

'Mike?'

Hunt held out his hand to the big stallion, the superb beast she'd see Hunt on from her bedroom window. It crunched the small treat it had taken from Hunt's palm and then stood patiently while he slipped on the bridle. 'This is Mike,' he informed her.

'That's a very prosaic name for a gorgeous beast like that.'

'His official name is Lucifer, but he's far too sweet-tempered to be lumbered with that.'

A black mare shooed the sheep off and demanded her

share. Laughing, Cia held out her hand and while the mare chomped the nuts she stroked her nose and said, 'I've heard of cats and dogs living together happily, but I don't think I've ever come across horses and sheep.'

'It happens reasonably frequently here. Horses and goats often do well together, and my father once trained a gelding that refused to be parted from his best friend, a donkey.' Hunt hefted the saddle onto his mount and bent to fasten it.

'That's Rio,' he said, watching as the mare tried to coax more treats from Cia. 'Do you want to ride her?'

'Yes, please.'

He bridled the mare, pandering to her flirtatious overtures with a gentle stroke to her nose, before leading both mare and stallion through the gate.

He watched as Cia saddled her, then nodded. 'Need a hand up?'

'No, thanks.' Expertly she stepped into the stirrup and up and into the saddle in one lithe movement. The mare jibbed a bit, but Cia settled her with a competent hand and watched Hunt. Like her, he lifted himself easily into the saddle, then nudged his mount towards her. The combination of the big bay's height and Hunt's meant he towered over her.

Pertly, she said, 'I do know what I'm doing.'

'And now I know it too,' he shot back. 'Let's go.'

Hunt's station was beautiful, a massive chunk of land extending from the hills to the sea.

Gazing out from the edge of the escarpment that dropped down to the coastal plain, Cia looked her fill, finally sighing and turning to the man who watched her. 'You're wrong.'

Hunt's brows lifted. 'On occasion,' he said drily. 'What are you referring to?'

'You said that this didn't look like a Renaissance painting; it does. It's like the landscapes the Old Masters painted—it has an untamed air.'

'I'm surprised you remember.'

Cia suspected she remembered everything he had said to her.

After a moment he went on, 'The light's different, of course. In summer it hazes over, but the autumn rains always wash it clean.'

'It's so—empty,' she said quietly. 'Fresh and new and green. I can't even see a road—oh, yes, I can.'

'Those are farm races,' he told her. He sat back on the stallion and examined the land below him with keen eyes.

'It didn't occur to you to build on the coast?'

'Too inaccessible. The main road goes up the centre of the island.' He turned inland and pointed to a range of blue-purple hills. 'But one of these days I plan to build a new beach house—to replace the old shack at the bay.'

When he had children? Cia wondered, and was surprised at the complex mix of emotions that thought brought with it.

He looked entirely suited to this, sitting so easily on his horse, looking out over his land. 'Lord of all he surveyed,' she said unevenly.

He lifted an eyebrow. 'No, that's your cousin,' he said. 'Literally. But Hinekura is not as big as Dacia.'

'Dacia doesn't belong to Luka. It's a democratic monarchy, not a dictatorship,' she said defensively, shocked because it was the first time she'd thought of her cousin all morning.

In a piercing moment of understanding she realised that her love for Luka had faded like the memory of stars on a sunny day. For the first time since she'd been an adolescent, she felt whole again.

And naked. Loving Luka had been her safe harbour, she

thought desperately, gazing at the clumps of trees that dotted the grassy slopes below, the forested gullies and the straight lines of fences. But it had never been real love; just moon-beams and star-shine, lacking the tangible intensity of Hunt's touch on her skin.

And what she felt for Hunt wasn't love either. She glanced sideways, transfixed by the familiar shock of plea-sure. Everything about him stimulated her, from his strong profile to his lithe, casual grace, but it was a purely physical response, the earthy attraction missing from her feelings for Luka.

Perhaps one day she'd find a man who combined both tenderness and passion. But when she tried to imagine it, she could only see Hunt's face, superimposed over every-thing else as though his potent magnetism had stamped itself onto her innermost being.

With words like *dangerous* and *reckless* and *heady* flash-ing around her brain, she went on, 'Which reminds me—I forgot to email Luka and Alexa last night—I'd better do it when I get back. Can I just hook into your phone line, or will I need a special cord?'

Hunt's mount fidgeted as though an unwary hand had tightened the reins. 'I'll check it when I get back, but I imagine it will need a special cord. New Zealand is a long way from Dacia; we do things differently here.'

An odd tension pulled between her shoulder blades.

Then Hunt wheeled the big bay and said laconically, 'Time to go back.'

A warm wind, heavy with moisture, whipped across her cheeks as she followed suit. When the stallion lengthened stride into a gallop she let the mare follow, relishing the opportunity to satisfy some hidden, inner wildness with vi-olent action.

# CHAPTER NINE

BACK at the house Cia went up the stairs feeling a pleasant ache in her thighs and calves. It had been too long since she'd ridden—and it would be too easy to fall in love with this beautiful place.

After showering off the scent of horse, she changed into a pair of slim-fitting trousers and a shirt. The residual energy from the ride had leached away under the warm spray; yawning, she slipped on her watch, then looked at Luka's star, glimmering in the depths of her jewel sack. She almost put it on, using it as a talisman against something she didn't dare identify.

But it was ridiculously superstitious to think that Luka's gift could protect her from...

From what? In the mirror her mouth tightened into a straight line and her eyes slid sideways, lashes drooping to hide her thoughts.

She wasn't falling in love with Hunt. Oh, she was attracted to him—

'You want him,' she said brutally, watching the words form on her mouth, the way her lips suddenly looked full and provocative and eager. 'You're an idiot because you want him so much you can't think straight. He's invaded your mind, and when he touches you it's like being struck by lightning.'

And it was the same for him. Inexperienced she might be, but she recognised the very sensual challenge in his eyes. Trying to ignore the heat kindling in the pit of her stomach, she combed back her hair and picked up the drier.

133

'So what are you going to do about it?' she asked the woman in the mirror as she went through the routine of drying her hair. 'Run away? Or give in and get him out of your system?'

If she stayed at Hinekura she'd end up making love with him. It was as inevitable as the setting of the sun and the rising of the moon.

Which did she fear most—sating this fierce hunger of the senses, or starving it? Of course running away could pitch her into the middle of a media frenzy.

Her teeth savaged her lip until another yawn took her by surprise. Wistfully eyeing the elegant, comfortable daybed, she chose a book from the bookcase—one with coloured photographs of Northland—and stubbornly sat down in an armchair. She'd give herself ten minutes of calm repose, and then she'd go down.

But she woke to a darkening sky and the pricking of faint stars through the fabric of twilight. Stunned, she shot to her feet, then had to grab the back of the chair as her head pounded.

Five minutes later, after splashing her face vigorously with cold water, she opened her door to see Hunt coming towards her, lithe and silent in the rapidly darkening passage.

'Are you all right?' he asked abruptly.

'I seem to have a lingering case of mild jet lag,' she told him with a wry smile that hid, she fervently hoped, her shivering pleasure at the sight of him. 'Another night's sleep will cure it, but I'm surprised. I've never had jet lag before.'

'You've never flown to the other side of the world before.' Frowning, he examined her face, a merciless scrutiny that made her feel as though she'd been caught out in a lie. 'It's a natural response to having your internal clock thoroughly disorganised.'

'I'm sorry to be such a boring guest,' she said with dignity.

His eyes kindled. 'Boring? Far from it, princess.'

'Don't call me that,' she said between her teeth.

His eyes challenged her. 'What would you like me to call you?'

*Darling,* hope whispered wickedly. *Dearest one, my heart...*

'I've got a perfectly good name,' she retorted.

He gestured for her to walk with him. 'You've got a formal name, Princess Lucia, and a family name, Cia. I'm not family and I'm a New Zealander, which means I don't go for formality, so I'll call you princess. Would you like a drink before dinner?'

'Orange juice would be lovely,' she said stiffly, her throat dry.

Hunt put her into a chair on the terrace overlooking the stream, beneath one of the big market umbrellas that sheltered the outdoor furniture from both the heat of the sun and evening's softly drifting dew. The little stream chuckled by as small birds with bright beady eyes and tails like fans whisked silently around her, catching invisible insects in the soft, scented air. On the other side of the stream soft lights bloomed amongst the rocks, highlighting ferns and water plants.

'I'm surprised you don't have mosquitoes here,' she commented, accepting the long glass of juice Hunt handed her.

'Mosquitoes prefer stagnant water, and any that manage to make it get eaten by the fantails.' The lights picked out the arrogant blade of Hunt's nose, glowed warmly over the brutal sweep of his cheekbones and the determined jaw.

A fierce pang of need tore through her. Hastily she drank some juice and said the first thing that came into her mind.

'This is delicious—so sweet, with just a faint note of acid to give it zing.'

Heavens, she was babbling!

He directed a sardonic look her way, a look that tingled through her. 'It's a local product. Northland produces a lot of citrus—mandarins and oranges as well as limes and lemonade fruit and lemons. Tangelos too.'

'Lemonade fruit? What are they?'

As she settled back in her chair to listen to his brief rundown of the local delicacies, a deep, aching contentment seeped through her. It didn't banish the tension; in an odd way it added to it. Desire she could understand; this sweet feeling of rightness was new, and, she suspected, even more dangerous.

But for those quiet minutes when the dusk fell silently around them, she listened to Hunt's deep voice with its excitingly raw undernote and pretended that she hadn't made love with him, that he didn't despise her, that they were two people who'd just met.

Later that night while she slept, she finally let her long-held love for Luka slip away like a skein of silk, waking in the morning to memories free of pain.

Bewildered, bereft, she lay still in the big bed, listening to the dawn chorus. How had it happened? Until yesterday morning she'd been utterly convinced she loved Luka, yet this morning it had gone, as though one night had cut the past cleanly off from the present.

Not one night, she thought with a flash of apprehension. Hunt. Like a conqueror he had moved in and taken over, sweeping away everything but her response to his powerful presence.

But he's far too dangerous to love, she thought, and firmly squelched the little thrills of anticipation that chased each other down her spine.

She had believed that once she was able to escape her unrequited feelings for Luka, she could be happy. Instead, as she got ready for the day, she was torn between apprehension and a smouldering excitement.

So she should have been relieved when Hunt told her over breakfast, 'I have to go to Perth in Australia for a few days.' He sounded curt and businesslike.

Cia fought back a corroding sense of loss. 'When do you leave?'

'In half an hour.' He glanced at her, eyes cool and opaque as lapis lazuli. 'There's some work you could do if you want to, but don't feel obliged. It's not very important, and you don't look as though you've got rid of that jet lag yet.' He drained his coffee and stood up. 'Don't ride until I come back.'

Tilting her chin, she replied with syrupy sweetness, 'Would you like me to get Marty to do lifeguard duty whenever I swim?'

'A good idea,' he tossed back succinctly. 'Did you hear from Dacia overnight?'

Irritated, she picked up a piece of toast. 'Yes. They're fine, and Alexa sends her love.'

He nodded and looked at her. 'Goodbye. Don't come out,' he said, and left the room.

Offhand described him exactly, she thought, wondering why she was so angry.

She forced food down her throat, drank a cup of tea, and stubbornly stayed in the breakfast room. She heard him call out to Marty, the slam of the door, and then the sound of the Range Rover. Stupid tears clogged her eyes as she sat in the sunny room and waited until the noise of the plane engine coming towards the house brought her to her feet.

She shot out onto the terrace and waved crazily, laughing

when the pilot waggled the wings on the turn south to Auckland.

Marty came in as she walked back through the doors. 'So the house loses its heart,' the older woman said with a smile. 'You haven't had enough to eat, surely?'

'I'm fine, thank you,' Cia told her brightly, and went into the office to type the few letters Hunt had left for her.

Although she missed him so acutely it felt as though she'd lost a limb, she settled into life on the station with real pleasure. She walked around the homestead area, acquiring a follower in the shape of an alert, half-grown farm dog called Bonzo who took a fancy to her. She waved to men on horseback or driving tractors, stopped and talked to children on their way home from school, and helped women hang out the family wash on the clotheslines.

They were friendly and not in the least awed by her. It was a huge change from the constant attention in Dacia, and she revelled in it.

Yet each night in her lonely bed she knew she was spending each day listening for Hunt's plane to return.

'You're looking shadowy under the eyes again,' Marty said sternly on the third day. 'Go up and have a nap.'

Cia glanced out at the sunny day, but the tiredness that had bedevilled her since she'd landed in New Zealand dragged her down. 'This wretched jet lag,' she complained cheerfully. 'Next time I cross the world I'm going to do it in stages.'

'Might be an idea,' the older woman agreed noncommittally.

An hour later when Cia woke, she felt the difference in the house immediately. In fact, she thought, bouncing off the bed, she'd probably heard the plane arrive in her sleep, because it was impossible for the atmosphere to change, yet she knew that Hunt was home.

A powerful cocktail of emotions fizzed inside her—eagerness, joy, excitement and something else she had no intention of examining. Humming a pop tune, she got into a pair of sleek trousers and a silk shirt, both the soft burnished topaz that went so well with her eyes and skin.

But when she came out of her room she was assailed by a piercing shyness. Her breath locked in her throat, she walked down the stairs and through the silent house. Hunt wasn't in the office; he wasn't on the terrace overlooking the little stream.

After a short hesitation she walked around under the wide overhang towards the courtyard with the swimming pool.

And there he was. Her heart contracted painfully.

From the shadow of the overhang she watched his strong arms cut through the water with such force it made her feel weak. The sun burned his bare shoulders copper, and the water darkened his hair into a slash of black as he swam length after length. There was something hypnotic about the powerful rhythm of his strokes, the relentless pushing of his body that shivered through her.

Her heart jumped when he finally stopped and climbed out of the pool in one strong, practised heave. Water streamed from him, outlining with loving precision his sleek, strong body as he dragged a towel off the back of one of the steamer chairs.

Only then did he look at her. Transfixed by his unsmiling scrutiny, she forced a smile and said lightly, 'Hello. How did the trip go?'

'Fine.' He rough-dried his head and shoulders, then dropped the towel. 'But I'm glad I'm home.'

He stooped and kissed her, and this time there was no holding back for either of them.

But Hunt lifted his head too soon, metallic blue eyes burning into hers. 'Made up your mind?'

Somehow all her cowardly caveats didn't seem important now that he was back. And her kiss had already answered him in the most basic way.

'Yes,' she said simply, reaching up to cover his heart with the palm of her hand. Its beat drove into the soft skin, heavy, regular, emphatic.

Hunt smiled, the intent, hungry smile of a lover close to triumph, but his voice was amused. 'Marty's in the house, so we'd better not startle her by heading up to a bedroom now.'

When Cia flushed he laughed quietly in his throat. 'But she'll be gone by six o'clock—it's her choir-practice night.'

Excitement rode her hard. 'Have you got any correspondence you want done?' she asked, adding demurely, 'To fill in time.'

Hunt covered the hand on his chest with his, pressing down so that the intoxicating rhythm of his heart mingled with the beat of her quickening pulses. 'No. Let's ride until she goes. It will help me to keep my hands off you.'

It did, but although they were careful not to touch each other, their eyes exchanged messages that wound the tension between them tighter and tighter until Cia thought she might explode with frustrated need.

Marty left them a superb dinner, which neither did justice to. After they'd stacked the dishes in the kitchen Hunt said starkly, 'I'd like to do this the romantic way and carry you up the stairs, but I don't dare touch you.'

Cia's smile trembled on her lips. 'I don't dare touch you, either, and although I'm sure love in the kitchen is incredibly wonderful, Marty might not approve.'

So they walked up the stairs side by side, tension smoking between them—a wild clamour of desire and certainty. This, Cia thought, was why she had stayed at Hinekura. She was free now, and this time there would be no regrets.

She'd spent the past few days—no, every second since they'd made love in the summer house in Dacia—craving Hunt. Her heart and mind had tried to lock him out, but her body had known better; with simple, primal insistence, it recognised its mate.

But once in her bedroom, she didn't know what to do. Bracing herself, she turned to glance up at him through her lashes. What she saw in his face made her drag in a jagged breath.

'Don't look so scared,' he said harshly. 'Somehow you've got under my skin and into my blood. I spent these last three days in a constant state of arousal, missing you, stopping myself from ringing you every ten minutes just so that I could hear your voice.'

It wasn't a declaration of love, but it would do for now. Beggars, she thought painfully, can't be choosers.

'At least you knew where I was,' she said.

He made a soft guttural noise in his throat and reached for her, crushing her mouth beneath his with passion enough to burn through her resistance and carry her defences by storm.

Shaking, so caught up in the moment that she couldn't think, Cia surrendered utterly to the demands of her own body.

'Hunt...' His name tapered away into a soft moan when he pushed away the silk of her shirt and kissed her breasts.

Sensation roared through in an all-consuming flood and she was lost; this time they came together with an untamed ferocity that shocked and excited her.

The first time they'd made love he'd led her by slow, sensuous increments to ecstasy. This time it was fast and fierce, a swift shedding of clothes, an eager, savage possession for both of them—her fingernails tearing into his shoulders, his arms fastening around her like iron bands, the bold masculine power of his big body as he drove into her, her urgent demands for satisfaction, until rapture rolled over them like a tidal wave, hurling them up on some unknown shore where the only thing that mattered was their mutual pleasure...

With the tremors from their explosive climax still shuddering through them, Hunt lifted himself onto his elbows and stared into her eyes as though he was trying to read her soul.

She met his gaze fearlessly. 'Did you prove whatever it was you were proving?' she asked in a voice husky with residual heat.

His mouth twisted. 'No,' he said. Then, 'Yes.'

'No and yes?'

'That you want me as much as I want you.'

She moistened her lips. A slow, sweet shudder of renewed energy ran through her when she saw the fire the tiny movement kindled in his eyes. 'And the negative?'

His eyes went dark. 'That you're no more able to resist it than I am.'

Was that what he'd meant to say? His kiss, tender and sweet, silenced the little doubter in her brain.

He said, 'I don't want to share you with anyone—we can take a few days off. Pack some clothes and we'll go down to the bach.'

She hesitated, then laughter swelled inside her. 'The shack you're going to tear down?'

'It's primitive but comfortable—nothing like the summer house in Dacia.'

A flicker of something in his midnight-blue eyes made her wonder if he was testing her. It didn't matter; sooner or later he'd realise that she didn't insist on luxury.

'I like the sound of comfort, and just you and me,' she

purred, and bit his shoulder in a thoughtful way. 'How long are we going to stay there?'

'Pack for several days.'

Joy burst inside her like a skyrocket. 'I'll be ready in twenty minutes.'

He stretched, a magnificent sight, and grinned. 'Is there a princess school where you learn to get ready in half the time of most women?'

Cia refused to acknowledge the slight chill his words produced. Of course he was accustomed to this. He knew how long it took a woman to get ready. 'I've always been like it.'

The bach was tiny and old, and primitive described it fairly well, but it was clean and the bed was huge and exceedingly comfortable.

This was important, because for the next four days they didn't move far from that bed. Each morning and night Hunt checked in with the homestead, but apart from that they spent all their time on or very near the small, white curve of sand with its huge overhanging trees whose name took her some time to learn to pronounce.

Hunt took her fishing; she teased him unmercifully when she caught one bigger than his, but he got his own back when she had to admit that she didn't know how to cook them. They swam. They talked, they discussed the elderly books that lived in a makeshift bookcase, and other books they'd read, and they found they could sit in silent companionship.

But mostly they made love.

Cia had never thought of herself as a passionate woman; her love for Luka had been almost entirely without any sexual feeling, but Hunt showed her how sensual she could be. In a continual glow of excitement, her system became sensitised to him until he had only to look at her in a certain way, gleaming eyes narrowed, a half-smile on his lips, and she was ready for him.

One night, lying near to sleep in his arms, she thought a little sadly that he was so *good* at this. He'd taught her the earthy delights of foreplay, the languid eroticism of afterglow, the screaming ecstasy of white-hot speed and power, and the simmering, unbearable pleasure of making love with slow tenderness. He was an expert.

As though he sensed the bleak way her thoughts were heading, he nuzzled her ear and murmured, 'I have this fantasy of making love to you when you're wearing nothing but jewels.'

'I don't have many jewels,' she said, laughing a little. 'If we were in Dacia we could borrow some emeralds, but not here.'

He laughed too, and kissed a certain intensely excitable spot below her ear. 'How about the diamond star?'

She froze, and he lifted himself on his elbow, looking down at her with lazily amused eyes. 'No?'

'No,' she said, adding with a different little laugh this time, one that was brittle and artificial, 'Luka gave it to me. I'd feel embarrassed—a bit like having a photograph of your mother on the bedside table.'

He laughed at that and eased her on top of him. 'I see.'

Thoughts roared through her head, but she couldn't stop any for long enough to catch one. In that frozen moment she realised that she had made the unforgivable mistake; she'd fallen in love with him.

And as his hand stroked the length of her spine from her neck to the dip at her waist, and the familiar craving smouldered into life, she understood that she'd never really loved Luka.

He was the past; Hunt was the present. She refused to speculate about the future.

Tomorrow they were going back to the homestead after the most wonderful four days of her life. Cia didn't want to leave; if they stayed there in the bach, in this precious limbo, nothing could harm them or the fragile relationship they'd forged.

Of course they couldn't; Hunt had a series of meetings in Auckland. He'd asked her if she wanted to go with him, but she'd said no. She didn't want the world intruding on their idyll.

But she was bright and cheerful when they went back to the homestead, and she waved him goodbye with a smile.

And then she waited for him to come back, sleeping long hours to catch up on the sleep she'd lost in his arms.

He came back five days later. Cia was swimming when she heard the plane come in low overhead, and such joy tore through her that she sank to the bottom of the pool. She burst out into the sunlight to the sound of the engine changing as it touched down. Excited and euphoric, she hauled herself out of the water and dashed into the cabana to shower and pull on her clothes.

'You're too late to go up to the airstrip with Ben,' Marty called out as Cia ran into the house.

'I know. I was swimming.'

The housekeeper appeared at the door. 'He'll be glad to be back. That trip to New Caledonia to see an old friend came out of the blue.'

'Mm.' She was radiant, so glad that Hunt was back she suspected she might not be able to hide her delight.

Humming, she ran up the stairs and leaned out so that she could see the Rover come up the drive.

Hunt looked a bit drawn, the angular features more sharply defined than usual, and after greeting her he apologised briefly for having to work until dinner. Disappointed,

Cia read and walked in the garden, eagerly looking forward to the night.

Long before the evening ended her delight had dwindled into foreboding. She couldn't put her finger on any change in Hunt, but the lovely closeness they had achieved at the bach had gone, evaporated like morning dew. When he looked at her it was with burnished, unreadable eyes, his control very evident.

Had he met someone else?

Painfully she hid behind her princess mask, produced small talk, discussed the news and told him small events that had taken place while he was gone.

Eventually he said, 'You're looking a little tired, so perhaps you'd like to go to bed now.'

'I would,' she said politely, and got to her feet. 'Goodnight.'

Ten minutes after she'd closed her bedroom door behind her someone knocked on it. She shrugged her dressing gown on over her slim cotton pyjamas and went across. Hope burst into bloom again; Hunt was standing there with a small parcel in his hand.

'Yes?' she said remotely.

'I need to talk to you.'

She stood back to let him, watching uneasily as he walked over to the bed and dropped the parcel on the coverlet. Long and slim, it looked—it looked like a jewellery box. A cold stone lodged just under her breastbone.

Then he turned and faced her, his face dark and austere. 'The friend I went to see in New Caledonia,' he said deliberately, 'was Édouard Lorraine.'

Cold with foreboding, Cia repeated the name in a flat voice as though she'd never heard it before.

'Maxime Lorraine's father,' he said.

'I know.' She swallowed and said, 'How—how is he?'

Hunt shrugged. 'He's married again. I went to his wedding.'

She stared at him and he sketched a brief, cold smile. 'He's a pragmatic Frenchman; he wants someone to leave his money to. And Maxime is dead. He's married a woman young enough to bear him children.' He paused. 'So tell me about Maxime Lorraine.'

Panic kicked beneath her ribs. 'I don't know what you mean.'

'Was he your lover?' He examined her face with the scalpel sharpness of a scientist checking out a hypothesis.

Cia's legs threatened to fold underneath her, but self-preservation stiffened them. He was too tall—darkly intimidating, he towered over her. 'We were not lovers, and why do you want to know about him?' she asked distantly.

A black brow lifted in silent disbelief. Ignoring her question, he said, 'So what did you feel for him?'

Cia told him the truth. 'I liked him.'

'*Liked* him? Poor bastard.' When she didn't answer he didn't attempt to hide his disbelief. 'Why did he think you were going to marry him?'

Talking to him was like climbing an icy, implacable wall. Her hands clenched at her sides. 'He—I hoped...' Her tongue seemed too big for her mouth and she didn't know what to say. Stiffly, she stated, 'You have no right to cross-question me.'

'You hoped that he'd be a good husband? A good lover? That he'd keep you in the style to which you've become accustomed? That he'd be so delighted to have snared a princess for a wife that he'd be complaisant when you sought out other men to slake that hunger of yours?'

The swift, cruel accusations cut her pride to shreds, but she kept her head high. 'I hoped that I'd learn to love him,' she said remotely, the words an admission of culpability.

'But it didn't happen. And his proposal came as a surprise—we weren't close enough for that.'

'If that's true, why was he so shattered by your rejection that he went off on some stupid expedition to the Congo?'

Cia's head came up proudly. 'My rejection had nothing to do with that—he planned to join the expedition whatever happened.'

'Not according to his father.' His eyes blazed with coldly furious fire.

It seemed treachery to be talking like this of poor dead Maxime. He'd fretted because his father didn't treat him as an adult, as a leader of men. The expedition had been his chance to prove that he could meet his father's expectations.

'He and his father loved each other, but I gathered they weren't close,' she said quietly. 'Perhaps you'd like to tell me exactly what this has to do with you.'

'Why didn't you fall in love with him?'

'Nobody can fall in love to order!' she shot back.

'Especially not if they're in love with someone else—someone out of reach,' he said with merciless scorn. 'You loved Luka when you caught Maxime in that sensuous snare you weave so well, and you loved him when you made love with me. You're in love with him now.'

Her skin went hot, then chilled as a cold sweat broke out on her brow. She thought she might be going to be sick, but she fought the sensation and said proudly, 'I'm not. Even if I was when I met Maxime, what does that have to do with you?'

'Just this,' he said between his teeth. 'I don't like standing in for another man. In fact, I can think of nothing more humiliating than to realise that the woman I'm in bed with is imagining another man in my place.'

## CHAPTER TEN

'No!' THE word burst from Cia. She finished fiercely, 'It wasn't like that.'

Equally fast was Hunt's brutal rejoinder. 'But you're in love with him. No wonder you stopped wearing his star when you decided to make love to me.'

She made a weary gesture, and said, 'I thought I was in love with him. I know now that I wasn't.'

'Why? Because you came to orgasm in my arms?' he demanded contemptuously.

Cia had no answer. To try and convince him would only mean revealing how she felt about him—and pride forbade that. Nausea gripping her stomach, she said woodenly, 'All I can say is that when we make love I didn't then and don't now imagine anyone else. Of course I can't prove it. And who told you that I was in love with Luka?'

'Édouard again,' he said crisply. 'Apparently Maxime worked it out from something another woman said when he was in Dacia. Although Édouard believed that who you love is your business, when he realised you were living here with me he decided to make sure I knew what I was up against.' He smiled with a merciless lack of humour. 'He thought I might be in love with you.'

His tone told her just how ludicrous he found that. Pale and shaken, Cia said quietly, 'Will you go now, please?'

'Not before you've opened your present,' he said, indicating the package he'd dropped on the bed.

'I don't want it. Please take it and go.'

'It's yours,' he said negligently. 'I'd hate you to leave

this place feeling that you'd wasted your time.' He picked up the package and stripped the wrapping from it. It was a jeweller's box; he flicked it open and drew out a rivulet of golden flames and ice, a chain set with diamonds and an exquisite pendant.

He held it out. 'These are Australian diamonds—better suited to your colouring than emeralds, or the stones your cousin gave you. Consider it payment for services rendered.'

Cia's stomach lurched. She flung him a desperate look, then turned and raced into the bathroom, only just getting there in time. A few seconds later in the midst of her misery, she heard him follow her in. Wretched as much with humiliation as the misery of being sick, she closed her eyes.

When the paroxysm had passed, leaving her white and shivering, Hunt sat her down with alarming gentleness and wiped her face with a damp, warm cloth, waited while she cleaned her teeth, and then picked her up and carried her back to the bed, already pulled back.

The diamond chain, she was thankful to see, had gone.

'Stay there,' he said. 'I'll get you something to drink.'

'I don't want anything,' she whispered.

But he brought a jug of water and a glass, only leaving when she'd sipped some of it.

Exhausted, Cia slept as though she'd been slugged with an iron bar, waking to another bout of nausea. Tension—or a stomach bug? At least while she was throwing up, she thought with black humour as she showered, she wasn't grieving over the shattered remains of her affair with Hunt.

But when she came back into the bedroom he was halfway across her room, frowning and angry. He stopped and watched her cross to the bed, his eyes keenly watchful.

Once she'd pulled the blanket up he said quite pleasantly, 'Do you have anything to tell me?'

Cia croaked, 'Like what?'

'Marty says you're still sleeping a lot of the time.'

Anger and a bitter premonition licked through her. 'I didn't realise she was a spy.'

'She's concerned about you.' His casual tone was countermanded by the keen intensity of his gaze.

'I've obviously been incubating this bug,' she said uncertainly. 'I'll get over it.'

'You're not drinking coffee or wine.'

Cia shrugged. 'More grilling, Hunt? When I'm by myself I don't drink alcohol.'

'But you usually drink coffee. You haven't since you've been here.'

She shrugged a little more deeply. 'For some reason the smell has made me feel a bit queasy, so I've been drinking tea. What has that got to do with anything?'

'For some women, it has quite a lot to do with being pregnant.'

Shock hit her like a blow to the heart. She stared at him, saw icy anger in his eyes and groped for composure, but could only stutter, 'P-p-pregnant?'

'Sleepiness and an aversion to caffeine are common indications. Were you on the Pill when we made love that first time?'

The colour drained from her skin. 'No, but you used protection—'

'They've been known to fail,' he said lethally. 'I assumed you'd be sensible enough not to make love unless there was no chance of conception.'

*Sensible?* At that time all thoughts in her head had been swamped by desire.

He went on, 'However, I'm not blaming you—I should damned well have known better.'

Cia had thought the long-drawn-out agony of loving Luka

had inured her to pain; now she discovered that she hadn't known anything about it at all.

A cold, still pride came to her aid. She said woodenly, 'This is pure supposition. I don't feel—'

'If it's mine, you can't be much more than a fortnight pregnant, so I don't suppose you *feel* anything. I suggest you find out.' Contempt hardened his voice.

She had once thought he'd make a bad enemy. She'd been right. Squaring her shoulders, she said icily, 'If—and that's a huge if—I am pregnant, believe me, it's yours!'

His face closed down. 'Rest here for the time being. Once the shops are open I'll send Marty into town to collect a pregnancy kit.'

Heat flamed across her skin. She said angrily, 'You don't need to involve her in this. She's done enough, surely, by telling you of her suspicions. I'll get one myself—'

'And run the risk of someone recognising you?'

'No one knows who I am,' she returned, head held high.

His face didn't relax. 'How do you know?'

'I've been walking around here talking to your people, and no one's said a word.'

'They know,' he said shortly. 'New Zealanders tend not to make a big fuss of visiting notabilities.' He forestalled her next objection. 'And anyone in town will certainly know who I am. Marty is utterly trustworthy. Once we know, we can take it from there.'

With the taste of ashes clogging her mouth, Cia leaned back into the pillows and closed her eyes.

'Are you all right?'

'No,' she muttered, opening her eyes to glare at him. 'Will you please get out of here and *leave me alone*?'

He said, 'I'll get Marty to bring you up some dry toast.'

'I don't want anything, thank you.'

But Marty brought up the toast anyway, with tea and

some orange juice. 'Hunt said you like it,' she said calmly, putting the tray on Cia's lap. She straightened up. 'I'll be up in an hour or so.'

By then the stone in Cia's stomach had assumed giant proportions, but she forced herself to drink the tea and some of the juice and nibbled at the toast.

Hunt was right; it did make her feel better, so much so that an hour or so later she got up and dressed. Going downstairs wasn't an option; unable to order her thoughts or emotions, she paced the floor of the room, her mind racing as futilely as a trapped animal.

After an hour or so of merciless worrying, another knock on the door heralded Hunt again, big and aloof and determined.

'Yes?' she asked stonily.

He handed her a paper bag. 'And I want to see the results.'

Humiliation burned like a hot brand through her. Her chin came up and she looked at him unwaveringly. 'Go to hell,' she said pleasantly. 'If I'm pregnant it's none of your business.'

'If you're carrying my child,' he bit out, 'it's definitely my business. Now get into the bathroom before I forget the deference due to a princess.'

So angry she couldn't articulate any of the words that burned her lips, Cia shut the door in his face.

For long moments she stood just inside, hands clenched at her sides while she thought vengefully of all the things she'd like to do to Hunt Bloody Radcliffe.

But eventually she walked into the bathroom, staring with acute distaste at the package. Eventually she forced herself to open it and read the instructions, noting bleakly that the makers promised accuracy even if the pregnancy had been established only a couple of weeks.

If she was pregnant, she vowed, she'd go back to Dacia and have her baby there. The chilling distaste in Hunt's tone still rang in her ears. Eating her heart out for Luka had been much safer than this foray into the wilder regions of love.

Slowly she followed the instructions and waited, staring at the stick until it changed colour. Her hand touched her waist, and she looked up to meet Hunt's eyes in the mirror, chips of ice in a face so angular that it could have been carved from stone.

She demanded harshly, 'What do you think you're doing?'

'I'm making sure you're all right,' he said, clipping each cold, terse word. 'Tell me the truth—whose child is it?'

'Yours,' she said, white-lipped and shaking.

'How do you know?'

Goaded into fury, she spun on her heel and threw at him, 'Because until I slept with you I was a virgin!'

'Not according to Maxime,' he said.

'Then Maxime lied. I don't care what he told you, or his father, or whoever he told all this to; I did not make love with him,' she said unevenly, fighting raw desolation. 'Now, let me past. I need to start organising things.'

'What things?' he asked dangerously, stepping back.

'I'm going back to Dacia.' With chin angled high she looked him straight in the eyes, her own blazing. 'You can forget about me—if I am pregnant, I won't tell anyone that you are the father. I can look after my child myself. It won't ever be alone.'

He followed her into the bedroom. 'You're damned right it won't,' he said grimly, 'because you and I are getting married.'

For a split-second hope burst into glory in her heart, but one glance at his face killed it. It tore her to shreds to refuse him when she so passionately wanted to accept everything he offered, but she couldn't marry a man who despised her. 'No.'

'Yes,' he said.

Cia saw his complete determination, and her heart quailed. She said quietly, 'Why would you marry me if you don't believe the child is yours?'

'I do believe it's mine,' he said quietly.

Her skin tightened. 'You won't believe anything else I say—why would you believe this?'

'Because if you were a virgin when we first made love, it has to be mine.'

She met his sceptical scrutiny with as much composure as she could. Time seemed to stretch as she lost herself in the frigid depths of his eyes. A bird called outside, a wistful little trill that ached through her.

He said curtly, 'The evidence backs it up.'

'What evidence?'

'Your passion seemed to surprise you, and you showed a charming, and very appealing lack of experience. I was pretty sure you were a virgin until you climaxed.'

Colour stung her skin.

He said with dry irony, 'I'm sure I don't have to tell you that a woman rarely comes to orgasm her first time, so I dismissed my suspicion for a more likely scenario—that you were relatively inexperienced, but I'd given you your first orgasm.'

'I see,' she said tonelessly. 'In other words, the evidence of your own eyes. But you have no evidence that I led Maxime on then dumped him when I realised his father was in financial trouble.'

'I have pretty good evidence.' He shrugged. 'You, to start off with. I've been fairly constantly in your company over the past couple of weeks—enough to know that you under-stand business. Wedding or not, you'd have known about

Lorraine's situation—and it was pretty grim for a week or so. But Édouard Lorraine wouldn't lie to me, and he told me what Maxime had told him.'

She stared at him, a cold knot of angry fear contracting in her stomach. Only the composure of long practice enabled her to say without expression, 'And you believe that Maxime wouldn't lie to his father.'

He was watching her with the flinty ruthlessness of a man who had fought his way to the top. 'Once Édouard told me that you are in love with Luka, it all made sense. You realised that it was no use hoping for Luka to wake up and see that he had the perfect wife in you, so you decided to cut your losses and do what any sensible, penniless princess would do. You looked around for a husband to keep you in the manner to which you've been accustomed.'

Stiff-lipped, her heart frozen and dead in her chest, she said, 'And when it looked as though Maxime wouldn't be able to keep me in luxury, I got rid of him? It does make sense—if you're a cynic.' Another thought struck her. 'Tell me, Hunt, do you think that I was actively trawling for another rich man to *keep* me? Do you think I decided you'd do as well as Maxime?'

He shrugged. 'It doesn't matter now. What matters is that you are pregnant with my child, so you're going to marry me.'

'Just like that?' she asked dangerously. 'You'd marry a woman you believe to be a fortune-hunter, a woman in love with another man?'

He came across the room in a silent lunge, all primitive hunter. Cia flinched, but stood firm when he said in a silky voice that lifted the hairs on her skin, 'I can deal with your childish crush on Luka. I'll make sure that you don't miss him too much.'

She opened her mouth to insist that she no longer loved

Luka, but primitive self-preservation closed her lips without letting a word escape. Once he knew she loved him, he'd take advantage of it. Later, when this icy serenity had shattered, she'd feel pain, but at the moment she was in control.

His eyes narrowed. 'You were going to say?' he prompted, his voice a rough purr.

'Nothing.'

He lifted her chin and subjected her to another probing examination. 'And I'll make sure you don't want for anything,' he said deliberately.

'That's an inducement?' she asked, white with temper.

'Most people,' he said with insulting confidence, 'would agree that my money in return for your title and social position is a fair exchange.'

'Do you believe that?'

This time the silence rang with unbearable intensity. Hunt didn't move when he said, 'Do you?'

'No, but don't worry.' The words rocketed out like bullets. 'I can introduce you to several very eligible princesses—and quite a few of the lesser ranks—who'd be happy to marry you on that basis.'

Sickened, she picked up the diamond chain she'd found in the drawer of the bedside table. She turned and in a spasm of rage and grief, hurled it at him. He made no attempt to catch it, so the exquisite insult dropped onto the carpet.

Each painful word ringing with conviction, she said, 'I'm not going to marry you. You don't trust me enough to believe me—why should I believe that you'd be a good husband to me and a good father to a child? If there is one.' She angled her chin in a movement as unconscious as it was defiant and walked towards the bathroom.

He stopped her easily, big hands holding her until she gave up the struggle and settled for glaring at him.

He said, 'I'm sure you have a list of princesses a mile

long, but none of them have tiger eyes and skin as cool and fragile as silk—until it heats under my touch—and none of them make me laugh and infuriate me. And no other woman has ever got between me and my work.'

'And no other woman has let herself get pregnant by you,' she said wearily.

'Don't cry.' He kissed her eyes, closing them on the tears aching behind them, and then kissed her mouth and the point of her chin, and her temples.

It took every ounce of will-power she possessed to stay wooden in his grip. When he let her go she said rigidly, 'You can make me want you, but I'm not going to marry you.'

His eyes were as lethal as the blue sheen on a gun barrel. 'You'll marry me,' he said in soft intimidation. 'You'll marry me if I have to force you to. I know what it's like to grow up a bastard; the innuendoes still turn up now and then in the gossip columns. I'm not going to put any child of mine through that.'

Ghost-white, she turned towards the daybed. Hunt saw her falter and took the three steps to catch her, holding her slender, rigid body close. In spite of everything, his hormones roared into life, primitively possessive, fiercely determined to protect her even when she didn't want it.

And she didn't want it. Her eyes glittered like the golden gems she'd flung at him, but at least colour had returned to her skin.

'I am not going to faint,' she said between her teeth. 'I have never fainted in my life, and your baby—if there *is* a baby—isn't going to make me start.'

Although his grin was reluctant, it was definite, a flash of white teeth in his tanned face, an unwilling glint of admiration in the blue eyes. He tightened his arms around her, bringing her closer.

Temptation hammered at the bars of her will, already weakened by his admission that he'd been hurt by his situation as a child. Resisting it, she said abruptly, 'Let me go.'

But the words emerged only a few decibels above a whisper. She repeated them, more strongly this time.

'All right,' he said, and lifted her to her feet, carrying her effortlessly to the bed.

Eyes enormous, she stared at him. He looked down at her, and the anger in both pairs of clashing eyes faded, to be replaced by something far more dangerous. Cia felt the soft rasp of her breath in her lungs, and the swift tattoo of her pulses as frustrated sexual tension brought with it a surge of passion.

She repeated desperately, 'I'm not going to marry you.'

'So what will you do? Run back to Dacia and steal Alexa's thunder in a storm of gossip?' he returned, setting her on her feet.

Cia bit her lip, stopping only when she saw his gaze rest on her maltreated mouth. 'I haven't yet decided,' she said reluctantly, adding, 'And this—possible pregnancy—might just be a false alarm.'

'It's certain enough for me,' he said caustically. 'I don't know how you feel about it, but the last thing I want for any child of mine is for it to grow up in a fanfare of controversy and media speculation.'

Hunt watched the colour drain from her lovely face, leaving stark cheekbones and trembling lips. He'd deliberately chosen to remind her of the media frenzy that had followed her mother's death. Ignoring a twinge of sympathy, he pressed her further. 'If we're going to put a stop to that, we need to get married fast.'

She shook her head. 'I'll go to Dacia.'

Hunt had had enough. Coldly furious, he said roughly,

'The international gossip circuit will go crazy about the fall of the Ice Princess—especially as Alexa is also pregnant. You can never go back.'

He was right, damn him. She couldn't do that to Luka and Alexa. Steadying her voice with an effort, she said, 'Hunt, you can't force me into this or persuade me, or run roughshod over me. I need to think, and you're stopping me.'

The anger he'd been keeping under control threatened to break free. When she blocked him out by closing her eyes, he said fiercely, 'Look at me.'

She shook her head, but her eyes flew open when he sat down on the bed.

With sombre forcefulness he said, 'We have several things going for us, princess—passion, and a certain compatibility of mind.' He touched her waist lightly, then withdrew his hand. 'And a child.'

Oh, he knew how to persuade!

When she stayed silent he went on uncompromisingly, 'If we don't get married soon, the world will know that we conceived the baby before our marriage. Because of who you are—who I am—there will always be gossip.'

She hesitated, then gave a reluctant nod.

He said explosively, 'I wish to God we were just a couple of ordinary people off the street, able to live ordinary lives.'

'No you don't,' she said, shaking her head. 'You could have chosen a life like that, but you wanted more.'

The flicker of emotion in his expression was swiftly concealed by his frown. 'Ordinary or not, I'd still want you,' he said and stood up, towering over the bed. His deep voice hardened. 'And I'd want my child to grow up confident that its parents cared enough for it and each other to marry, to give it roots.'

Cia's heart twisted at the thought of the boy who'd never

known his mother, wasn't even sure that the man he called father was the man whose genes made him what he was.

She said crisply, 'I've got more than roots—I've got a whole blasted tree stretching back a couple of thousand years. It means nothing. My father used his title and his charm to con my mother into marrying him. Her pedigree was almost as long as his, but when the marriage disintegrated she used drugs to stop the pain, and eventually killed herself with them. You don't need roots, you need good basic foundations; the important thing is the person you turn out to be. Your father taught you well, but he had excellent material to work with.'

'My child isn't going to grow up not knowing who it is,' he said impatiently. He turned and looked at her and smiled—pure devilry, both calculating and sexy as hell. It set her heart flipping. 'Fortunately I have the weapons to make sure that you'll enjoy being my wife.'

When she didn't answer he bent, and as her eyes widened and she said sharply, 'No!' he traced a snaking line from the corner of her mouth to the centre of one expectant breast.

His touch was so light that Cia glanced down, thinking dazedly that flames should be licking along the path his finger took.

Dry-mouthed, her body craving more, she managed to say, 'And I'm not going to be seduced into this, either. It's not just you and me—if I am pregnant, we have to think of the child. An unhappy marriage is sheer hell for children— trust me, I know.'

'Then we'll have to make sure it's not unhappy,' he said coolly. 'Has it ever occurred to you that falling in love with your cousin was an attempt at replacing your own useless father with one who loved you?'

Startled, she looked up into a face both angular and controlled. 'It could have been,' she admitted, wondering what other thoughts were circulating in the clever, analytical mind behind his angular features.

'And Maxime Lorraine?'

Her teeth clamped on her lip. 'I did use Maxime,' she said, low-voiced. 'I liked him so much—and it's no excuse, but I was vulnerable and unhappy.'

Knowing she wouldn't make a difference, she tried to make Hunt understand. 'I hoped—I thought I could will myself into loving him. But I didn't feel—when he tried to make love, I realised I couldn't. So I told him it wasn't—that I was sorry.'

Hunt got up and walked across to the window. 'What sticks in my craw,' he said with cutting contempt, 'is the cold deliberateness of your behaviour.'

That hurt, but he was right. 'You can't make me feel worse than I already do about it,' she said wearily.

'And your timing.' He laid out his objections with the merciless dispassion of a judge. 'How could you have been unaware of his father's business problems? Lorraine's is one of the biggest conglomerates in France.'

'I told you, Alexa and I were organising a wedding,' she flared, indignation driving her. 'It was a madhouse, and I simply didn't have time to read the papers and watch television.' She paused, then said bluntly, 'I can't prove I didn't know, just as I can't prove that I was a virgin.'

Silence spun a web of tension between them. Hunt didn't move; he didn't believe her.

Shrivelling inside, she added, 'But it wasn't my refusal that drove him to Africa; he had every intention of going on that expedition. He knew his father wouldn't approve, but he was excited about it; he thought it would prove once and for all that he was his father's son.' Poor Maxime.

Hunt was staring out of the window, broad back and shoulders making a perfect male triangle above his narrow hips and long, muscled legs. Every waiting nerve strung taut, Cia took in several deep breaths and tried to regulate her pounding heartbeat.

She didn't ask for love from Hunt, but if he didn't believe her, she couldn't marry him. Trust was imperative in any relationship. Especially marriage, she thought wretchedly.

'None of that matters now,' he said indifferently, turning to look at her with burnished blue eyes, emotionless and fully in control. 'I'll make an appointment for you to see my doctor as soon as possible. But even if there's only a fifty per cent chance that you might be pregnant, you're marrying me.'

Under the shower a few minutes later, Cia let the hot water play over her shivering body. He meant it.

For a weak, stupid few moments she let herself fantasise that she could be content with crumbs rather than the feast. Better a loveless, practical union than never seeing him again.

After all, plenty of her ancestors had coped with an arranged marriage. The sex would be fabulous, and in time he might learn to trust her.

Colour heated her skin and with a short, vicious twist of her wrist she turned the water on to cold and endured it for several depressing moments until she flicked it off and got out.

'Is that a pig I see flying above the trees?' she wondered aloud, rubbing her hair.

And then she wept a little into the soft towel, because she'd made a terrible mess of everything.

She'd just emerged from the shower when someone knocked on the bedroom door. Nausea roiled in her stomach. Now that the adrenalin surge of quarrelling with Hunt had faded she was exhausted and ominously weepy.

After more deep breaths she went across and opened the door. Without preamble, Hunt said, 'I have to leave. There's been a forestry fire in Sarawak with deaths—I need to be there.'

'How many deaths?' she asked quickly.

'About ten so far.' His hard features clamped into a harsh mask. 'This is a joint venture with several villages—if I'm on the spot I can see what's needed, and I have the power to get equipment into the area. Cia, I need your promise that you'll do nothing about this situation until I come back.'

'You have no right to ask that of me,' she said quietly, hurting.

He hesitated, then asked with rough insistence, 'Please.'

One of the disadvantages of loving someone, she discovered, was the desire for them to be happy. With a touch of bitterness, she said, 'I'll stay.'

He nodded and looked at her, and then reached for and kissed her, a hard, swift kiss that frightened her with its savage intensity. 'I'll see you when I get back,' he promised, and left her.

Half an hour later she waved at the plane from the terrace with an inward shiver.

The fire—a huge jungle fire set by subsistence farmers—made the following night's news, as did Hunt's arrival with specialist firefighters and aid. Cia watched greedily, then went to bed with that dart of fear working itself further into her heart.

The next day she decided she needed to go into the nearest town to buy a few odds and ends. When she told Marty, the housekeeper looked surprised.

'Make a list out,' she suggested, 'and I'll order them for you.'

Cia said pleasantly, 'I'd rather get them for myself, thank

you. I could take the Range Rover—I have an international driver's licence.'

Marty gave her a wary glance. 'I don't think Hunt would approve of that,' she said quickly. 'Our roads are pretty bad. I'll go in with you.' She glanced at the clock in the huge kitchen. 'Give me half an hour.'

Not only did she drive Cia in, she stayed with her while she did her shopping. Cia realised with a sick fury that Hunt had given orders for her not to be given a chance to leave.

It reinforced every fear she had about the marriage; Hunt's lack of trust chilled her. It was bleakly ironic, she thought when they'd arrived back home, that she had gone from not being able to have the man she wanted, to an offer of marriage from the man she loved—one she didn't dare accept.

Hunt came back four days later, after the fire had been doused with no further loss of life. Cia was cutting flowers for a vase when she heard the sound of the plane. Her heart lifted in sudden, fierce joy.

The plane came in from the sea and swung over the house. As it disappeared below the bush to land, she heard an alteration in the sound of the engines.

Her heart stopped. And then she heard the crash.

# CHAPTER ELEVEN

AFTERWARDS she could never remember what she did between hearing the rending, tearing groan as metal tore into the grassy paddock, and finding herself in the Range Rover with white-lipped Marty and Ben.

Marty said harshly, 'They'll be all right. They're both brilliant pilots.'

No one answered. The vehicle shot out from under the trees and up towards the airstrip. Well before they reached it they could see the plane, lying on its side in the grass with one wing torn free. Several people were clambering around it.

'Landing gear failed,' Ben muttered. 'At least it didn't flip. They should be all right—they'll have been wearing seat belts.'

Cia didn't dare let hope grow to more than a tiny flicker in case he was wrong.

As soon as the Rover stopped she forced open the door and jumped out. Snatches of images flashed across her brain as she ran towards the crippled plane—one of the shepherds talking into a mobile phone, a man racing back towards her, a woman standing with her hands pressed to her mouth.

When Cia had almost reached the plane she was grabbed and held. 'Let me go,' she panted, struggling with her captor.

'Miss, I can't. There's avgas leaking—you mustn't go any closer.'

Her heart stopped and for a second the bright grass and the wrecked plane whirled in hideous confusion. Ferocious blinking stopped the rotation. 'You can let me go,' she told him, swallowing hard. 'I'll stay here.'

He released her with alacrity, stepping back as Ben came to stand beside her. Gruffly he said, 'You can't do anything until they've got them out of the plane.'

She stared at the fuselage with straining eyes, searching for signs of movement. 'Are they—are they all right?' she croaked.

'They're both alive,' the man who had stopped her said, his voice sympathetic, 'but Hunt's in and out of consciousness. The ambulance is on the way, but they have to get them out of the plane as quickly as they can.'

He didn't say why, but she knew. The stench of leaking avgas was thick in her nostrils. She clamped down on rising hysteria and began to pray.

Ben said soothingly, 'If it had been going to burn it would have happened as soon as they crashed.'

*Hunt,* she thought painfully, willing him to be all right, to be barely hurt. Oh, God, please...

She spared a moment's prayer for the pilot, but her mind immediately jumped back to Hunt. A man roared up in a van and others dragged out poles that they assembled into a stretcher.

The pilot emerged first, shaken but conscious. It took them much longer to get Hunt out, but eventually he was flat on the stretcher. Men grabbed the poles and carried him across the strip, Marty jogging beside with a medical kit.

Rigid with anxiety, Cia made her way through the small group of people and stopped beside the stretcher, looking down at Hunt, lying strapped in. Blood streamed across his face from a wound on his forehead and beneath the deep tan, his skin was pale.

'It looks worse than it is,' Marty told her bracingly. 'He can feel his toes so it's pretty unlikely that he's got anything wrong with his spine, but the straps are just in case. Don't worry; he's as tough as old boots.'

'I know.' Cia's voice was low and bleak; the thought of all that splendid strength crushed and confined to a wheelchair made her feel sick.

Hunt opened his eyes and looked straight at her. The quiet hum of the onlookers faded; Cia smiled down at him and said, 'Well, you certainly know how to make an entrance. Next time, a little less drama, OK?'

Someone laughed, and Hunt lifted a hand. She knelt beside the stretcher and took it in both of hers. 'You've probably got a beastly headache; don't talk,' she said, and held his hand to her cheek.

She stayed like that until the ambulance arrived, only moving away to let the nurse stabilise him. A short distance away the pilot sat wrapped in a silver survival blanket. Pale and sweating, still in shock, he managed an awkward smile when she came across.

'How is Hunt?' he asked.

'He's going to be fine,' Cia said, desperately hoping she was right. 'How are you?'

'All right—I didn't hit my head.' He shrugged. 'I'm trying to work out what went wrong.'

'Don't worry about it—you got both of you down more or less undamaged.'

'Yeah, I suppose, your maj—highness?' He looked embarrassed.

Smiling, Cia said, 'My name is Lucia.'

He lifted his head and listened, then said with relief, 'Here comes the chopper.'

It came in with noisy brashness, disgorging people who went about their business in a kind of organised rush.

When Ben came across Cia asked in a thin voice, 'What's happening?'

'They'll take them to the hospital to check them over,' Ben said.

'I'm going too.' Cia ran across towards the big chopper, determined to stay with Hunt.

A pleasant woman barred the way. 'I'm sorry, but—'

'I want to be with Hunt,' Cia said fiercely. 'I'm his fiancée.'

From behind Marty said, 'I'll drive down with some clothes and your bag—you might need to stay the night if he's got concussion.'

'Thank you.' Cia ducked. Wind from the big rotors whipped around her as she ran across and scrambled into the helicopter.

Hunt still lay with his eyes closed, the cut above his eye bruising fast. Cia knelt and breathed his name, and to his astonishment his eyes opened. His lips formed her name and her tears started to fall softly and silently.

Carefully, she laid her head down against his and whispered, 'It's all right. Everything's going to be all right.'

'Can you hold her hand?' the woman who'd tried to stop her asked Hunt.

He lifted his and clasped Cia's, and the woman laughed. 'And you can wiggle your toes so there's not much wrong with you,' she said. 'But we'll make sure everything's in good shape before we send you home.'

Cia held his hand all the way down to the hospital. Once there she huddled in a waiting room while he went through interminable procedures, grateful when Marty and Ben arrived because talking to them took her mind off the appalling things that could have happened.

When at last she was allowed into Hunt's room, he turned his head to watch her come in.

'How are you?' she asked, suddenly shy.

'According to the medics, I'm fine. Slightly bruised, but not anything to worry about. How are you?'

Her lips trembled. 'All right now you're all right.' She blinked back tears. 'You look very interesting. That bandage across your head is an improvement. Did you have stitches?'

'Only those butterfly sutures.' He swallowed and she found a glass of water and held it to his lips.

After he'd sipped some he said ironically, 'Not the way I'd planned to return.'

'No. Don't ever do it again.'

A minor stir at the door heralded a doctor, who introduced himself and then said, 'Well, you and the pilot were pretty fortunate. We're keeping you both for observation tonight, but there's nothing wrong with either of you. If you have a good night your fiancée can take you home tomorrow morning.'

When he'd gone, Hunt said, 'Fiancée?'

Colour streaking her cheeks, she muttered, 'They weren't going to let me on the helicopter.'

'Ah, I see.' He was silent, and then he opened his eyes again. 'You're crying.'

'I'm allowed to be a bit emotional,' she said inadequately. 'I love you.'

He was silent for a long time, then said, 'A fine time to tell me.'

'It doesn't matter. Go to sleep.'

His head must have been throbbing because he closed his eyes again and drifted off. Cia allowed Marty and Ben to take her to a motel, where she spent much of the long night wondering what had possessed her to blurt out her greatest secret.

Hunt, sporting a rakish patch on his forehead and a formidable air of self-possession, was ready to head home when they arrived at the hospital the following morning. With Marty and Ben in the car as well, Cia didn't expect him to refer to her confession of the night before, but as he sat silent and aloof beside her on the drive back to Hinekura, the joyous expectancy she'd woken with faded.

She wanted him to go to bed when they got home, but he refused. 'I'm fine,' he told her, brows drawing together. 'You, however, look a bit pale. Why don't you rest?'

'I might do that,' Cia said. Clearly he was in no mood to talk.

In her room she stood by the window and looked out across the garden she'd come to love. Once again she felt torn, but this time between a tremulous hope and a cold dread.

She'd nailed her colours to the mast; there was no going back for her. Hunt knew she loved him.

The rest of the day passed uneasily; the media had got wind of the crash, so Marty spent a lot of time fending off telephone calls. An insurance agent came and went, and an inspector of aviation accidents flew in by helicopter to check the plane. The farm manager was closeted with Hunt for most of the afternoon; during dinner he spoke firmly of nothings, and went to bed early.

At breakfast the next morning he said, 'Would you like to go to the beach today?'

Cia looked up. 'The beach?'

Was he going to tell her that he didn't want to marry her after all? A sensible marriage was one thing; marrying a woman who'd admitted she loved you was a much more complex situation.

'We'll take the Range Rover and some lunch and spend the day there.'

Apprehension churned her stomach. 'It would be lovely,' she said sedately. 'I'll drive, though.'

This produced the first smile she'd seen since he'd come back from hospital. 'Fine. You might as well learn how to drive on the left.'

Once she got behind the wheel, Hunt explained the gears and gave her directions, his cool pragmatism easing the spiky tension between them. While she was concentrating on negotiating farm roads, she could banish the thoughts that chased fruitlessly through her brain.

It took almost an hour to get there, and as she braked to a stop outside the little bach she remembered with aching clarity the days—and nights—they'd spent there.

'You're a good driver,' Hunt told her.

Smiling, she switched off the engine. 'Thank you. Still no headache?'

He gave her a quizzical glance. 'Not today.'

Still formal, still somewhat detached, as though warding off any intimate conversation, yet his eyes kindled whenever he looked at her.

Because the simple pleasure of being alone with him was enough, she forced herself to relax in the warmth of the sun, to walk along the warm sand beside him and breathe in the sharp tang of salt and talk inconsequentially.

Back by the car they spread out a rug and sat down on it. And Hunt said quietly, 'When did you realise that you were no longer in love with Luka?'

Cia had been picking out the pattern on the rug with a stem of dry grass. It wavered in her hand, but she said steadily, 'I wasn't ever *in* love with him. I know that now. Love killed my mother, so I chose someone unattainable.'

'Safe,' he said.

Yes, he understood. She nodded. 'I always knew that he'd never love me as a man loves the woman he wants.'

'But when he married Alexa you were desolate.'

She flushed. 'I wasn't ready to admit that I was too scared to trust any man enough to fall in love with him!'

'So you chose Maxime, whom you didn't love, because he was safe too.'

'At least I didn't go through with it—I'd have made him utterly wretched.' Cia glanced at him, and then glanced away again. 'I pray he didn't let himself die because he was unhappy—'

'Very few young men in the prime of life allow themselves to die of a broken heart,' Hunt said brusquely. 'The expedition wasn't well organised. When it ran into trouble they had very little medication left—not enough to get him through a bout of fever.'

'Did his father tell you that too?'

'Yes. I dropped in to see him on my way back from Sarawak. While he was dealing with Maxime's estate he discovered that Maxime funded the expedition, so he'd contacted an expedition member, who was much more forthcoming than the official account had been.'

She should have felt relieved that she'd been vindicated, but she still grieved for the laughing young man who had been such fun. Over the lump in her throat, she said, 'His death was such a waste.'

'But not your fault.' He waited then said with an abrupt change of subject, 'I'm sorry for putting you through that scene.'

She moved uncomfortably. 'I understand why you were so angry.'

'Nevertheless, I had no right to subject you to such a confrontation. And not realising that you were pregnant is no excuse.' Leaning back on his elbows, he watched her from hooded eyes. 'You didn't go to bed with him; why did you go to bed with me?'

'Because I couldn't stop myself,' she said honestly. She

flushed, but met his eyes. 'I despised myself because I was convinced that Luka was the love of my life, yet I wanted you desperately.'

Eyes intent, Hunt said, 'That's sex, not love. The two are not necessarily connected.'

Cia's heart contracted. Somehow she had to convince him that as well as wanting him she loved him.

'I know the difference,' she said, dropping the grass stem to loop her hands round her knees. 'Meeting you—making love with you—made me realise that what I felt for Luka was a child's hero-worship. I didn't *want* to accept that because I felt such an idiot for suffering all those years for some unrealistic dream. Of course I love him—but not the way I love you.'

'You think you love me because I gave you your first experience of sex. It's good—hell, with you it's bloody fantastic!—but don't fool yourself that it's love,' he said indifferently.

His cool, judicial words stripped the last, hidden, shameful thread of hope from her. This, she thought desperately, is the most important conversation I've ever had. She paused, searching for words to explain how she felt. 'I know the difference. I wanted you before I loved you. That might make me a freak, but it doesn't make me stupid.'

'You're not a freak,' he said bluntly. 'You're an intensely passionate woman with a thing about control.'

'Listen to who's talking!' she returned childishly.

He was watching her with hooded eyes that concealed everything but glittering blue sparks.

Controlling a kick of panic beneath her ribs, she said, 'When you were on Dacia you took over my mind; I couldn't think of anything but you, where you were, what you were doing—I was so aware of you my skin hurt and my brain buzzed! I really enjoyed being with you, I loved the way we talked, and I felt renewed, a different person.'

She got to her feet and walked across to the nearest po-hutukawa, tracing its furrowed bark with her forefinger. 'As for confusing sex with love—the day before yesterday when we drove up to the airstrip thinking you'd been killed, I wasn't worrying about how much I'd miss the sex!'

Hunt was silent, and she thought bleakly, *He doesn't believe me. He'll never believe me.*

And she knew that marrying him would kill some essential part of her. She said quietly, 'Hunt, it's no good. I saw what an unequal marriage did to my mother; I'm not going to let it happen to me.'

From behind her Hunt drawled, 'You're stronger than your mother ever was. And in this, princess, you have no choice. If you don't agree to marry me I'll contact the first tabloid I can and feed them details of our relationship—including the fact that you spent so many years in love with your cousin.'

She froze. 'You wouldn't.'

'I don't imagine either Alexa or your cousin would enjoy the resultant uproar,' he said implacably. 'Nor would the baby when it's old enough to realise what happened.'

Cia knew he was tough, had accepted that he was formidable and determined, but his ruthlessness appalled her. She remembered the horror of her mother's death, the avid interest, the mobs of journalists yelling her name and the flash of cameras. To her horror tears gathered in her eyes and began to spill over onto her cheeks.

'Why won't you believe me?' she blurted as she scrabbled for her handkerchief, so angry she could barely speak. 'What makes you so smugly sure that you can read my mind and my emotions? What do you want me to do to prove it to you—give you my heart's blood? I refuse to be black-mailed into marriage.'

She scrubbed her eyes and gulped, hauling up the last remnants of self-control.

Apparently unmoved, he said, 'When did you fall in love with me?'

The sound of the tiny waves sweeping the beach provided a peaceful background to the conversation, a bitter contrast to the turmoil that fogged her brain and clogged her thought processes.

'You walked through the gate at the airport and started being snide and sarcastic and I thought, Who does he think he is? I don't believe in love at first sight, but I was running scared from that moment, because my world changed when you walked into it.'

'I know the feeling,' he said harshly. 'I saw the woman who'd driven Maxime Lorraine to his death, and my first thought scared the hell out of me. I wondered if I was rich enough to have a chance. I've never felt such abject need, and I resisted it with everything I had.'

'There is nothing abject about you!' she snapped.

'Cia, what I'm trying to tell you—and making a pig's breakfast of it—is that all this angst isn't necessary.'

She didn't hear him move, but his arms around her were hard and purposeful, and the heat of his body surrounded her, sapping her strength and fogging her brain. He didn't try to turn her, but kissed the tingling back of her neck and murmured, 'Love, sex, whatever—we have more than that to forge a relationship from. If we don't set our sights too high, we can make a decent marriage.'

Shaken and desperate because she wasn't getting through to him, Cia felt something inside her snap. 'I've little taste for ritual humiliation,' she said in a low, passionate voice.

'I'm sorry you think that marriage to me will be humiliating, but you'll do it just the same, if I have to drag you to the altar,' he promised, his level voice utterly convincing. 'That's a given, princess. So is the fact that I'll be faithful, and the best husband and father I can be. Why is it so important that I believe you love me?'

'I don't know! Pride, I suppose—and because I'm not a child. I know how I feel.' In frustrated impotence, she clenched her fist and punched the trunk of the ancient tree.

Hunt moved like a hunting leopard, snatching her hand and cradling it in his own. 'Stop that!' he commanded, and as though driven, lifted it and kissed the reddening skin.

Cia's eyes filled with tears again. 'I don't usually bawl all the time,' she wept.

On a goaded note, Hunt said, 'It's all right. Don't cry—don't cry, damn you.'

His arms tightened around her and although the temptation to lean against his big body and accept his support was almost overwhelming, she resisted.

'You make me so angry!' she snarled into his shoulder.

'I can see that.' His voice sounded shaken. 'No, don't hit me.'

'I wasn't going to!' She gulped again, and this time gave in, surrendering to the strong haven of his arms with a sense of such profound homecoming that she knew she'd never be free of him.

He said in a wry voice, 'Right from the beginning, I was sure that hiding under that cool, very English, very royal princess there was a volatile Latin.'

And he lifted her, carrying her back to the rug. Still holding her, he sat down, and tucked her comfortably against him.

Tears drying miraculously, Cia glowered at him. 'So every chance you got you tried to dig her out.'

Hunt acknowledged the accusation with a sardonic smile.

'Only to find that your patrician self-control seems pretty damned shatterproof except when we make love.'

Heat arrowed through Cia, tempting, hugely seductive. *I'm going to give in,* she thought fatalistically.

He paused and when he spoke she sensed that he was picking his words carefully. 'This has all happened far too quickly. We've known each other less than a month, and neither of us have been thinking straight, but when that plane came down I could only think, *I'll never see her again.* And I knew I'd go down into death in rage and desperation.'

Tears ached at the back of her throat.

'Stop fighting,' he murmured, his mouth tracking across her forehead. 'We'll make a good marriage—I want you and our baby to be happy.'

When she opened her mouth to speak he kissed her parted lips, and as the sweet, familiar hunger burst into flames inside her she surrendered, as she would always surrender to Hunt because she loved him.

Although they made love with a powerful energy fuelled by the adrenalin left over from their quarrel, Hunt was infinitely tender, until she tantalised him into taking her without finesse, his raw sexual drive sending her into that welcome place that was theirs alone.

Much later he smoothed a long tress of tangled hair back from her face. 'We need to get married as soon as possible.'

She hesitated, then accepted her destiny with a faint, bitter regret that she had better get used to, because it would be with her for the rest of her life. 'But first we should make sure that I am pregnant.'

'Even without the test, I'd know you're pregnant.'

'How?'

'There's a glow about you, a softer kind of radiance,' he said with calm certainty. He pressed a line of kisses across her waist. 'And once I'd got rid of the idea of jet lag, your sleeping habits are a giveaway.'

Lifting her with him, he sat up and cuddled her against him, resting his cheek on her hair. 'I suggest we marry in Dacia. That way Luka can make sure it's not a media circus. Here, if news gets out, we might not be able to stop helicopters from buzzing the ceremony.'

Her cheek warm against the hard muscles of his chest, Cia shuddered. 'I'd like to be married there. And I think it should be private.'

He kissed her eyelids closed. 'I'll marry you in the biggest, most elaborate wedding you can organise, if that's what you want.'

'No thanks,' she said smartly. 'I've discovered the values of privacy while I've been in New Zealand. But if we are married in Dacia, Alexa's pregnancy means nobody would be surprised at a small wedding.'

'I don't care if the whole world knows you're pregnant,' he said, the words deep and quiet in his throat. 'In fact, some primitive male part of me feels like shouting it out to everyone at the top of my voice. I want you and our child safe and secure and with me.'

Eyes brimming with tears again, she touched his face. 'You'll be a wonderful father. I hope I'm not going to sob my way through this entire pregnancy!'

'Hormones,' he said with a laugh. 'Come on, let's get back to the homestead and finalise some plans.'

That night, just before she went to sleep in his arms, Cia wondered again if she'd sold her soul to the future. As sleep pulled her under, she decided that it was done; there could be no going back. Hunt might not love her, but he wanted her and the child she was now sure rested under her heart, and she had time on her side. He wouldn't abandon them as her father had abandoned her and her mother; his word was his bond.

Three weeks later they were married in the small chapel at the Old Palace. Luka gave her away, and Alexa made a charming matron of honour; the only other people in the chapel were friends and the closest members of her family.

Afterwards they drove through streets filled with cheering, petal-throwing Dacians to the Little Palace, where they held a reception for local worthies followed by an informal lunch.

Alexa went up with Cia to help her change and said when they were alone, 'I don't need to ask if you're happy—you're positively shining with it.'

'I feel great.' Cia removed the small emerald tiara from her head. She'd never wear it again; it belonged to the women of the Dacian royal family, and she was now Mrs Hunter Radcliffe.

Her heart sang.

Alexa laughed. 'I notice you no longer seem to mind the way Hunt calls you princess,' she said slyly.

'I rather like it,' Cia admitted.

'I imagine you would, the way he says it! It's terrific that our babies will be so close in age,' Alexa remarked, skilfully removing the exquisite lace train that fell gracefully from the back of Cia's silk chiffon dress, cut in neoclassical lines.

Cia froze. 'Oh,' she said. And then guiltily, 'I was going to tell you soon.'

Alexa hugged her. 'Luka and I guessed the minute we saw you. Luka's delighted, and so am I. Right from the start I was pretty sure that you and Hunt were meant for each other.'

Astonished, Cia said, 'Why? We have nothing in common!'

'This sounds hugely silly, but you look right together,' Alexa told her seriously. 'Like a really good photograph— something just fits.' She grinned. 'And of course we'd have had to be blind and deaf and stupid not to register the bolts of lightning between you! I'm so glad I convinced Luka not to object when you went to New Zealand with Hunt—he was all set to come over patriarchal and insist you go to England.'

Cia looked at her. 'Are you a witch?'

'I just want everyone to be as happy as I am. What are you going to do about your plans for university?'

'Hunt tells me that New Zealand has an excellent system for students who can't attend lectures,' Cia said. 'I'll use that.'

'Good for you.' Alexa kissed Cia's cheek. 'You deserve every happiness. Now, let me help you into that lovely suit.'

Cia nodded, but as she changed into her going-away outfit, she wondered if she was crazy to want more, when most other women would envy her.

She had made her bed; she had to lie in it.


The loud clatter of a helicopter coming in low overhead brought Cia to her feet. She walked across to the window of her office and looked out over a scene of seeming confusion. A quick glance reassured her that everything was going to plan; the marquee was up and although people were moving around, there was purpose in their actions. She examined the sky with narrowed eyes, but so far the forecasters had been spot-on; it wouldn't rain on the day of the annual Hinekura stud-bull sale.

Smiling, she went back to her lists.

A little later, a knock on the door whirled her around. 'Come in.'

It was Hunt, and as ever, her heart skipped a beat. 'I

thought it would be you,' she said, going swiftly towards him. 'Good trip?'

'Not too bad, but I'm damned glad to be home.' He held her close, his smile both tender and fierce. 'How are you both?'

'The baby and I are fine,' she said demurely, and pressed his hand against her thickening waist. 'Very active—she's heard your voice and is glad you're back.'

'Are you glad too?' Hunt tipped her chin so that he could see her face.

She nodded. 'Of course.'

'I love you, Lucia.'

In the five months of their marriage Cia had been happier than ever before. But now, with his eyes burning into hers and his hand on her waist as their child kicked with vigour, she rejoiced as the last citadel fell and Hunt let her see his real emotions.

'I love you too,' she said quietly.

He kissed her as though she was something rare and precious. 'I don't know why it took me so long to admit it. My father's experience with love didn't help; he loved my mother until the day he died—but even when I found that the more I have of you, the more I want, I wouldn't accept that it was anything more than a passionate friendship.'

Cia knew him much better than she had when they married. 'You said once that I had a problem with control,' she reminded him. 'You do too.'

'And once you admit you love someone, you hand over control to them.' He looked down at her face, his own stark with purpose. 'Every second of every day I spend with you tightens the chains. I want more from you than the rapturous welcome of your body and your quick, clever brain, your tact and discretion and brilliant organisation.'

She touched his cheek gently, the canary diamond of her

engagement ring flashing in the low winter sunlight. 'You've got it,' she told him, her voice soft. 'You've got everything.'

His arms tightened around her. With his cheek on her hair he said harshly, 'I love you so much, my darling, my dearest girl, my princess. You've warmed my cold heart and my life. Each morning I wake up and I think, She's here and we have the rest of our lives together, but I've never told you because it gave you such power.'

'What made you decide to do it today?' She was so happy she could barely articulate the words.

'I missed you so much, and I thought about the crash, and I knew I was just being a coward. You had the guts to tell me you loved me; I wanted you to know.' Eyes gleaming, he looked down at her. 'So, my heart's delight, will you forgive me for being so damned stubborn?'

'You ask that of a woman who convinced herself she was in love with a man for about ten years and never once asked herself why she didn't want to make love to him?' She laughed. 'Forgiveness isn't necessary. Just don't ever stop loving me.'

'I swear.'

He kissed her, and then she said, 'Oh! I forgot to tell you—Alexa had her baby this morning. A big, bonny boy, and they're both well. Luka was over the moon.'

The telephone rang and she said something crisp in Dacian beneath her breath, disentangled herself and answered it.

Hunt watched her, amazed at the freedom finally saying those three words had given him. She was beginning to round out deliciously, and their baby was making her presence felt. He laughed out loud, thinking he could take on the world and conquer it for his princess. She looked up and the golden glow in her eyes filled his life.

Smiling, she hung up and came across, and he said deep in his throat, 'When I hold you, I hold all that's important in my life.'

'Ditto.'

Their child kicked her vigorously again, and they both laughed, and went out into their future together.

The world's bestselling romance series.

### HARLEQUIN®
*Presents*

**Seduction and Passion Guaranteed!**

## Mama Mia!

# ITALIAN HUSBANDS

They're tall, dark...and ready to marry!

Don't delay, order the next story in this great new miniseries...pronto!

### Coming in August:
**THE ITALIAN'S MARRIAGE BARGAIN**
by Carol Marinelli
#2413

### And don't miss:
**THE ITALIAN'S SUITABLE WIFE**
by Lucy Monroe
October #2425

**HIS CONVENIENT WIFE**
by Diana Hamilton
November #2431

Pick up a Harlequin Presents® novel and you will enter a world of spine-tingling passion and provocative, tantalizing romance!

*Available wherever Harlequin books are sold.*

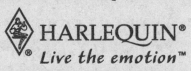

### HARLEQUIN®
*Live the emotion*™

**www.eHarlequin.com**

HPITALH2

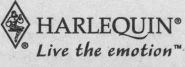

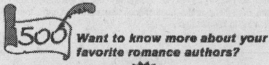

If you enjoyed what you just read,
then we've got an offer you can't resist!

# Take 2 bestselling
# love stories FREE!
# Plus get a FREE surprise gift!

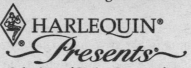

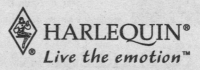

# Harlequin Romance®

*What happens when you suddenly discover your
happy twosome is about to be turned into a...family?*

*Do you panic?* • *Do you laugh?* • *Do you cry?*

*Or...do you get married?*

*The answer is all of the above—and plenty more!*

Share the laughter and the tears as these unsuspecting
couples are plunged into parenthood! Whether it's a baby
on the way, or the creation of a brand-new instant family,
these men and women have no choice but to be

## READY FOR BABY

*When parenthood takes you by surprise!*

Don't miss
***The Baby Proposal*** #3808
by international bestselling author
**Rebecca Winters**
coming next month in
Harlequin Romance® books!

Wonderfully unique every time,
Rebecca Winters will take you on an
emotional roller coaster! Her powerful
stories will enthral your senses and
leave you on a romantic high!

*Available wherever Harlequin books are sold.*

# HARLEQUIN®
## Temptation®

### When the spirits are willing...
### Anything can happen!

Welcome to the Inn at Maiden Falls, Colorado. Once a
brothel in the 1800s, the inn is now a successful honeymoon
resort. Only, little does anybody guess that all that marital
bliss comes with a little supernatural persuasion....

**Don't miss this fantastic new miniseries. Watch for:**

### #977 SWEET TALKIN' GUY by Colleen Collins
June 2004

### #981 CAN'T BUY ME LOVE by Heather MacAllister
July 2004

### #985 IT'S IN HIS KISS by Julie Kistler
August 2004

## THE SPIRITS
## ARE WILLING

*Available wherever Harlequin books are sold.*

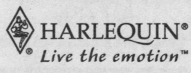

# HARLEQUIN®
### Live the emotion™